Lightning Reflexes

Clint didn't know where the gun came from but suddenly it was in Yates' hand. It must have been underneath the sheet on the bed.

Yates was bringing the gun to bear on Clint and the Gunsmith reacted by pure reflex. He pulled the trigger and his bullet punched a hole in Yates' chest. The man staggered back and fell to the floor. His foot tangled in the sheet and pulled it off the bed, where it covered half of him—the top half. As Clint watched, the man's blood began to soak through the sheet.

"Shit!" he said, and holstered his gun.

Also in THE GUNSMITH series

- MACKLIN'S WOMEN
- THE CHINESE GUNMEN
- THE WOMAN HUNT
- THE GUNS OF ABILENE
- THREE GUNS FOR GLORY
- LEADTOWN
- THE LONGHORN WAR
- QUANAH'S REVENGE
- HEAVYWEIGHT GUN
- NEW ORLEANS FIRE
- ONE-HANDED GUN
- THE CANADIAN PAYROLL
- DRAW TO AN INSIDE DEATH
- DEAD MAN'S HAND
- BANDIT GOLD
- BUCKSKINS AND SIX-GUNS
- SILVER WAR
- HIGH NOON AT LANCASTER
- BANDIDO BLOOD
- THE DODGE CITY GANG
- SASQUATCH HUNT
- BULLETS AND BALLOTS
- THE RIVERBOAT GANG
- KILLER GRIZZLY
- NORTH OF THE BORDER
- EAGLE'S GAP
- CHINATOWN HELL
- THE PANHANDLE SEARCH
- WILDCAT ROUNDUP
- THE PONDEROSA WAR
- TROUBLE RIDES A FAST HORSE
- DYNAMITE JUSTICE
- THE POSSE
- NIGHT OF THE GILA
- THE BOUNTY WOMEN
- BLACK PEARL SALOON
- GUNDOWN IN PARADISE
- KING OF THE BORDER
- THE EL PASO SALT WAR
- THE TEN PINES KILLER
- HELL WITH A PISTOL
- THE WYOMING CATTLE KILL
- THE GOLDEN HORSEMAN
- THE SCARLET GUN
- NAVAHO DEVIL
- WILD BILL'S GHOST
- THE MINER'S SHOWDOWN
- ARCHER'S REVENGE
- SHOWDOWN IN RATON
- WHEN LEGENDS MEET
- DESERT HELL
- THE DIAMOND GUN
- DENVER DUO
- HELL ON WHEELS
- THE LEGEND MAKER
- WALKING DEAD MAN
- CROSSFIRE MOUNTAIN
- THE DEADLY HEALER
- THE TRAIL DRIVE WAR
- GERONIMO'S TRAIL
- THE COMSTOCK GOLD FRAUD
- BOOMTOWN KILLER
- TEXAS TRACKDOWN
- THE FAST DRAW LEAGUE
- SHOWDOWN IN RIO MALO
- OUTLAW TRAIL
- HOMESTEADER GUNS
- FIVE CARD DEATH
- TRAILDRIVE TO MONTANA
- TRIAL BY FIRE
- THE OLD WHISTLER GANG
- DAUGHTER OF GOLD
- APACHE GOLD
- PLAINS MURDER
- DEADLY MEMORIES
- THE NEVADA TIMBER WAR
- NEW MEXICO SHOWDOWN
- BARBED WIRE AND BULLETS
- DEATH EXPRESS
- WHEN LEGENDS DIE
- SIX-GUN JUSTICE
- THE MUSTANG HUNTERS
- TEXAS RANSOM
- VENGEANCE TOWN
- WINNER TAKE ALL
- MESSAGE FROM A DEAD MAN

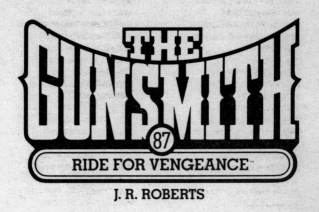

THE GUNSMITH 87
RIDE FOR VENGEANCE

J. R. ROBERTS

Lyons Public Library
448 Cedar St.
P.O. Box 100
Lyons, OR 97358

JOVE BOOKS, NEW YORK

THE GUNSMITH #87: RIDE FOR VENGEANCE

A Jove book / published by arrangement with
the author

PRINTING HISTORY
Jove edition / March 1989

All rights reserved.
Copyright © 1989 by Robert J. Randisi.
This book may not be reproduced in whole or in part,
by mimeograph or any other means, without permission.
For information address: The Berkley Publishing Group,
200 Madison Avenue, New York, New York 10016.

ISBN: 0-515-09961-9

Jove books are published by The Berkley Publishing Group,
200 Madison Avenue, New York, New York 10016.
The name "JOVE" and the "J" logo
are trademarks belonging to Jove Publications, Inc.

PRINTED IN THE UNITED STATES OF AMERICA

10 9 8 7 6 5 4 3 2 1

ONE

Clint Adams had been in Mercer, Texas, for only one day, but already he had made the acquaintance of Marcy Dobbs. Well, perhaps "acquaintance" wasn't exactly the right word, since they *were* in her bed together, and his head *was* buried between her thighs.

Marcy was a buxom blonde who worked in the saloon and had met Clint while he was playing poker. She had met a lot of men that way, and Clint Adams had met a lot of women, and soon as they both understood that they were free to go to her room and get better "acquainted."

Now Clint was busy bringing her to a climax with his tongue, licking the sweet, wet lips of her vagina while she writhed beneath him, pressing her butt into the sheets. When he found her clit and latched onto it with his attentions she made a sound in her throat that sounded like a scream just begging to get out—but it never did. She "suffered" her pleasure in silence, because she had screamed once, many years ago, and it had resulted in the death of the man she was with. Some damn fool outside the room had heard her and busted in with his gun out and accidently shot the gentleman who was doing just what Clint was doing to her now. That was a long time ago, and she hadn't screamed during an orgasm since. Sometimes, she could still see that poor fella's face . . . whatever his name had been. . . .

Later it was Marcy who was tucked between the legs of Clint Adams, her tongue avidly licking the length of him, wetting him good, and then taking him deep into her mouth and sucking him good . . . and loud!

Clint didn't mind the extra noise, though. In fact, he found that listening to her suck him made him even more excited, and when he finally exploded into her mouth, he bellowed like a wounded bull.

There had been no such incident in Clint Adams past, and when he wanted to yell—why, he just went ahead and did so. . . .

"I don't have many friends," Marcy told Clint later.

"I find that hard to believe, Marcy."

"Oh, there's men," she said, "don't get me wrong, but none of them wanted to be my friend—if you know what I mean."

Clint sincerely hoped that she wouldn't ask him at this point if he wanted to be her friend, because that had been the furthest thing from his mind when he came up here with her. What he'd wanted was to find out if her breasts were as firm as they looked, and if her mouth was as talented as he had the feeling it would be—and they were, and it certainly was.

Maybe, he thought, if he stuck around long enough they'd get to be friends.

Maybe.

Actually, he'd been on his way to Labyrinth, Texas, which was about a day's ride south, when he'd arrived in Mercer, with intentions of staying only one day. Now, however, with Marcy intent on becoming friends—there she was, down between his legs again—he just might decide to stay a few days.

RIDE FOR VENGEANCE 3

• • •

The following morning, while Clint and Marcy were getting to know each other all over again, Rick Hartman woke up in Labyrinth, Texas. Next to him was a tall, slender redhead who had almost no breasts to speak of, but she had the most gorgeous legs and butt he had run into in a month of Sundays, and the widest aureola he'd ever seen. Of course, it had been her legs and butt that got her invited into his bed. He hadn't seen those amazing nipples until later.

Now all he had to do was remember her name. Hmm, it had something to do with her hair, didn't it? Red? Scarlet? He looked at the bush between her widespread legs—she was lying on her back—and then said out loud, "Rusty?"

"That's me," the girl said, opening one eye. "I was wondering if you were going to remember."

"Of course I remember," Rick said, feigning shock at the idea that he wouldn't. "After last night I'd be a swine not to."

"Well, even if you didn't," she said, "there wouldn't be a whole lot I could do about it."

"You could bawl me out."

"Oh, no," she said, rolling over onto her side and propping her head up on one arm, "I learned a long time ago never to bawl out the boss. Of course, I also learned never to sleep with the boss, and here I am."

"If it will make you feel any better," Rick said, touching her right nipple with the forefinger of his right hand, "consider yourself under orders."

She leaned forward and said, "What is your next command, oh, Master?"

"Read my mind."

She closed her eyes and then snaked her hand down over his belly until she was holding his penis in her hand.

She had read his mind!

It wasn't until ten o'clock that Clint was able to get away from Marcy and go to have breakfast. He found a small cafe that served a decent plate of eggs and bacon and—even more importantly—a decent pot of coffee. After breakfast he'd send a telegraph message over to Labyrinth to let them know where he was. He usually liked to give them some idea, in case there were any messages for him.

He ate breakfast, thinking about the energetic Marcy and totally, blissfully unaware of what was happening at that very moment in Labyrinth.

TWO

Rick Hartman left Rusty Bonet—*not* her real name, naturally—in his bed and went downstairs to have his breakfast. There was no need for him to leave the building. Since he owned his own saloon—as well as several other businesses in town—he also had his own cook. He was in the middle of a huge breakfast of bacon, eggs, steak, biscuits, and coffee when he heard the shots from the street.

"Jesus, what now?" he said aloud.

"Want me to take a look, Boss?" T.C. asked. Not only was the big black man the bartender in the saloon, but he was the best cook in town.

"What is this, Dodge City?" Rick asked in disgust. "A man can't have his breakfast without somebody shooting up the town early in the morning? NO," he said, finally answering T.C.'s question, "I'll take a look myself."

He threw his napkin down and walked to the front doors. He unlocked them and then stepped out onto the boardwalk. He saw a man running toward him, and then heard several more shots.

"What's going on, Slim?" he asked, recognizing the man.

"Bank's being robbed, Rick!"

"Jesus," Rick said under his breath. "Where's the sheriff?"

There was more firing now.

"He and Ted are over there trying to stop 'em," Slim said, and kept running. That was just like Slim, running *away* from trouble.

Rick darted back into the saloon and shouted, "T.C., toss me that shotgun!"

T.C. obeyed. He went behind the bar, grabbed the shotgun from beneath it, and tossed it to Rick, who caught it with one hand.

"Boss, what's going—" he started to ask, but Rick was already gone.

Rick ran down the street toward the bank, aware of the heated exchange of fire that was now going on. From the sound of it, the sheriff and his deputy were outnumbered and could use all the help they could get.

As he came within sight of the bank he saw that the deputy was already down, lying in the street. There were half a dozen men on horses in front of the bank, and they were firing at one man, the sheriff, who had practically no cover. Even as Rick watched—and the rest of the town watched—the sheriff went down under a hail of bullets.

The bank robbers began riding down the street, and Rick had no time to get out of the way. He lifted the shotgun and let go with both barrels. He heard someone shout in pain, but then he was struck by something and white-hot pain shot through his body. He went down, and only felt the hoof of the first horse strike him in the head. After that, mercifully, he was unconscious.

"How bad is he, Doc?" T.C. asked.

T.C. was not the only person in the doctor's office waiting for the answer to that question. Rusty was there, along with the other three girls who worked for Rick, and they all had tear-stained faces—yes, even the big black bartender.

Doc Prentiss regarded them over the top of his glasses and said, "He's in very bad shape. He was shot twice. One bullet lodged in his left shoulder, the other in his chest. As if that wasn't bad enough, I don't know how many of those horses rode over him. To tell you the truth, it's a blamed miracle he's even alive."

"Oh, God," T.C. said. "He ain't gonna die, Doc, is he?"

The doctor looked annoyed, mainly because he felt so helpless.

"I've done what I can for him, but unless he gets stronger I can't try to remove the bullet in his chest. I got the one from his shoulder out, but that chest wound is too close to the heart. Is he gonna die? Hell, I guess I'd have to say that's up to him. Now why don't all of you people get out of my office and let me get back to my patient."

"He's right," Gloria Reynolds said, taking charge. She touched T.C.'s arm tenderly, knowning that he had known Rick much longer than any of them. "Come on, T.C. We can't do anything here."

"No," T.C. said, "I guess not. Let's go, girls."

They all left together and walked back to the saloon.

"I ain't gonna open today," T.C. said when they got there.

"Do you think that's what Rick would want?" Gloria asked. "He's gonna have doctor bills, T.C., and how's he gonna pay them if his place is closed?"

"I don't feel like working..." T.C. said helplessly.

"None of us do," she said, "but we got to."

At that moment a man came in the front doors and approached T.C.

"How is he?" he asked. His name was Tappy Nolan, and he was the telegraph operator.

"Not good, Tappy," Gloria said.

"Well, this came for him," Tappy said, handing the telegraph message to T.C.

T.C. took it, read it, and his eyes brightened with an idea.

"Who's it from, T.C.?" Gloria asked.

Instead of answering he ran out the door to catch up with Tappy Nolan.

If there was nothing *he* could do, maybe there was something the Gunsmith could!

When Clint Adams received the telegraph message from Labyrinth, he made immediate preparations to leave Mercer. Marcy, sorry to see him leave so soon, naturally understood.

"I guess we won't have time to become such great friends, huh?" she asked.

He took hold of her shoulders and said, "As far as I'm concerned, we're already great friends."

She smiled and raised her chin for a kiss. He gave her one, a chaste, friendly kiss, then mounted up and rode out.

By pushing Duke, his big black gelding, he'd be in Labyrinth before nightfall. All the message had said was that Rick had been seriously injured, and could Clint come as soon as possible. Clint did not even want to take the time to send another telegraph message asking how serious the injuries to his friend really were.

He'd be able to ask that question in person soon enough.

THREE

"How is he?"

Kyle Lanahan looked up at his older brother, Len, and said, "Not good, Len."

"Well," his brother said, "if he's gonna die I wish he'd do it soon. We've got to get moving."

"Len!" Kyle said, concerned that the injured man, Randy Hall, might have heard him.

"Tend to him," Len said, and went back to the fire where his brother—the middle brother, Will—handed him a cup of coffee.

"Little brother still playing nurse?" Will asked.

Len nodded, sitting next to Will. Len was 35 years of age, Will, 28, and Kyle was the baby of the family at 19.

"He brought Randy into the gang, I suppose he feels responsible."

"Only one responsible for Randy gettin' shot is Randy," Will Lanahan said.

"Tell that to Kyle."

The other two men in the gang were Sam Bigelow and Winston Yates. Yates was sitting across the fire from them while Bigelow was on watch.

"If he dies can we split up the money?" Yates asked.

"We split the money when we get into Mexico, Yates," Will said. "We told you that already."

"Why can't we just split it now and go our separate ways?" Yates wanted to know.

"Because we don't want you spending the money five minutes after we stole it, stupid," Will said.

Yates bristled and said, "Who you callin' stupid?"

"You, that's who," Will Lanahan said. "You wanna do something about it, now's the time."

Yates looked at Len Lanahan, and not at Will. Len was the leader of the gang, the one who kept the others in line because they were afraid of his gun.

"No, Will, I don't want to make something of it," Yates said.

"Then next time keep your mouth shut," Will said, and then added, "stupid!"

Yates gritted his teeth and stared into the fire.

"How long you think it will take them to put together a posse?" Will asked Len.

"I told you I checked that town out carefully," Len said. "One sheriff and one deputy, and we killed both of them. Before they can even think about a posse, they got to elect themselves a new sheriff. You know how long that's gonna take? I don't think we have to worry about a posse, Will. Not for a while, anyway, and by that time we'll be in Mexico."

"Not me," Yates said. "When I get my share I'm going to San Francisco."

Will started laughing.

"What's so funny?" Yates demanded.

"The thought of you in San Francisco. You gonna take a bath first, Yates?"

"What do I need a bath for?"

Will looked at Len and said, "See what I mean?"

"Lay off him," Len said, annoyed. He looked past Will to where Kyle was tending Randy Hall.

How the hell long did it take a man who'd been hit twice to die, anyway?

"I'm gonna relieve Sam," Len said. He tossed the remnants of his coffee into the fire and got up.

"You wanna play some poker . . ." Will was saying as Len walked away. If Yates was fool enough to be conned into playing poker for shares, he'd be broke before he even got his.

Len Lanahan was the gun hand of the three brothers. Will was the gambler. Kyle was still too young to decide what he was, but Len hoped he wouldn't end up being some kind of nursemaid.

Len went out to find Sam Bigelow. Bigelow and he had ridden together before, several times, and of all the men in this present gang, Sam was the only one Len would trust with his life.

That included Will and Kyle, his brothers. Will was too much of a loudmouth to be any real good in a fight, and Kyle was just too raw. Yates was a fool, and Randy Hall was no better.

Len wanted to talk to Sam Bigelow, because he was the only man in the bunch whom he could have a decent conversation with.

Sam was also the only other one of the bunch who'd ever killed anyone before. In fact, it was Len's shot that had killed the sheriff, and Sam Bigelow's that had taken care of the deputy. The others had been firing and hitting nothing until that fool with the shotgun had come along.

Idly, Len wondered who that man was, but then he decided that he'd probably never know that.

He couldn't have know how wrong he would be.

FOUR

It was almost dark when Clint Adams rode into Labyrinth. He put his horse up at the livery and did not stop to talk with the liveryman. He did not even go to the hotel or saloon. He went directly to Doc Prentiss's office.

"Doc," he said, entering the office.

Prentiss looked up from his desk and frowned. He was in his sixties and had slate-gray hair not only on his head, but also growing out of his ears.

"Who are you—wait a minute, I do know you, don't I? Adams, isn't it?"

"That's right."

"The Gunsmith, right?" the doctor said. "You're a big man in this town, right? Trying to put it on the map with your constant presence?"

"I don't know about that, Doc," Clint said. "I'm here to see how Rick Hartman is."

"He ain't good."

Clint approached the man's desk and put his hands flat down on it, leaning over the doctor.

"If you're intent is to intimidate me, Adams, forget it," Prentiss said.

"My intent, Doctor," Clint said calmly, "is to find out what kind of shape my friend is in."

Prentiss looked up at Clint, and then sighed.

"All right. He was shot twice, once in the shoulder, once in the chest. I've removed the bullet from the shoulder. I cannot remove the bullet that is lodged in his chest." The doctor stopped, as if expecting Clint to ask a question. When he did not, the man continued.

"He was also trampled by several horses, which inflicted a number of other injuries. None are life-threatening—a broken wrist, a broken collarbone, a possible concussion—but they are all debilitating." He stopped again, waiting for a question, but none came.

"In his weakened condition I do not believe he would survive an attempt to remove the second bullet. Therefore, I am waiting . . . to see if he gets stronger, or if he will simply die."

"And that's all you can do?"

"That's it."

"All right, Doctor," Clint said. "Thank you for your time."

"Er, you're welcome." As Clint started for the door the doctor said, "You don't ask a lot of fool questions, do you?"

"I try not to, Doctor," Clint said. "I assumed that you knew what you were doing, and what you were talking about. I only hope I'm assuming correctly."

Before the doctor could reply, Clint opened the door and left the office.

"Well," the doctor said, grinning in spite of himself, "I'll be damned!"

Clint's next stop was Rick's saloon, called appropriately, Rick's Place, which was open for business. He entered, saw T.C. behind the bar, and approached it.

"T.C.," he said.

The black bartender turned and when he saw Clint he smiled wanly.

"You made good time."

"Can you get away?"

"Sure. Gimme a minute."

He put a beer on the bar for Clint and then went to get a replacement for himself. He was back in a matter of moments, and said, "Come on, we'll use Rick's office."

Clint picked up his beer and followed T.C. to the back of the room, where they went through the door.

"Business looks good," Clint said.

"I know how it looks, Clint, like maybe we don't care and all—"

"Whoa, T.C.," Clint said. "That's not what I was thinking at all."

"Sorry," T.C. said, "I guess I'm a little edgy."

"Can you tell me what happened?"

"Have you seen the doc?"

Clint nodded.

"I heard his part, now I want to hear what happened before he got involved."

T.C. briefly told Clint about the bank robbery, and about Rick running out to help the sheriff and his deputy.

"I didn't even have time to ask him what was going on, or to run out and help him. By the time I got to him he was already down and they were gone."

"How many were there?" Clint asked.

"From the reports I heard, there were six."

"What reports?"

T.C. shrugged and said, "Just talk."

"Has anyone talked to the bank people yet?"

"I don't think so."

"Have you taken charge here?"

"Actually, Gloria has. I mean, she's the one got us all working to keep our minds off of . . . to keep us busy."

"Gloria?"

"Don't know if you know her," T.C. said. "In fact, I don't think you know any of these girls. They all been hired since the last time you were here."

"All right," Clint said. "I'll talk to the bank people tomorrow. You know the people in this town, T.C. What do you think are the chances of getting up a posse?"

"None," T.C. replied immediately. "These people may have lost their money, but there ain't a one who would pick up a gun to go after it, I can tell you that."

"Well, it's not so different from any other town," Clint said. "Besides, I don't have any official standing to put a posse together, anyway."

He stood up, leaving the beer mug on the desk.

"What are you gonna do?" T.C. asked.

"Like I said, I'll talk to the bank people in the morning and get descriptions of the bank robbers, and then I'll start tracking them."

"Alone? I'll go with you."

"No offense, T.C., but when was the last time you sat on a horse?"

"Not for a long time, but—"

"No, you'll do more good here, keeping the business going and keeping any eye on Rick. I'll be able to move faster if I don't take you. Understand?"

"I understand."

"I'll see you in the morning, then."

"Going to the hotel?" T.C. asked.

"Yes."

"Why don't you use the boss's room."

Clint looked up at the ceiling, as if he could see Rick's room from there and said, "I don't think so. I'll just stay in the hotel."

T.C. just nodded and watched as the Gunsmith walked out. He felt sorry for those bank robbers when Clint Adams caught up to them.

FIVE

The next morning Clint had breakfast in a cafe across the street from the bank. When he was finished, he ordered a second pot of coffee and drank it while keeping an eye on the bank. He wanted to go inside as soon as it opened.

He still had half a pot left when he saw the shades on the door go up, signaling that the bank was open for business.

He left the cafe, crossed the street hurriedly, and was the first one to enter the bank. He approached a young woman behind the teller's cage.

"Can I help you?" she asked with a professional smile.

"Yes. Were you working yesterday during the robbery?"

"I—uh, I'm not supposed to talk—"

"Look, if you were working I'd like to get a description of the men who robbed you. If not, then just tell me who *was* working and I'll talk to *them*."

"Uh, you'll have to talk to the bank manager—"

"Fine. Tell him I'm here."

"Just a moment . . ." she said, and hurried away from her window. He watched her knock on an office door and enter, and then reappear several moments later.

"Mr. Wolf will see you now."

"Thank you."

He went around the cage and walked past her, into the office. The man behind the desk was slender, with slicked back black hair and pince-nez glasses perched on his aristocratic nose.

"You may close the door, Milly."

"Yes, sir."

"I'm afraid she's still quite upset about what occurred yesterday," Wolf said to Clint.

"And you're not?"

The man frowned and asked, "Are you a depositor in this bank, Mr. . . . ."

"Adams, and as it happens, yes, I am, but that's not why I'm here."

"Let me assure you, Mr. Adams, that your money is quite safe—"

"My money is in the saddlebag of some bank robber who even while we speak is getting farther and farther away from here. I want to speak to someone who can describe to me what the men looked like."

"Why would you want that?" Wolf asked. "Are you a federal marshall?"

"No, I'm not—"

"Well, you're not the new sheriff. We haven't hired one yet, so—"

"Look, Mr. Wolf, I'm not a lawman, I'm somebody who wants to get on the trail of those killers as soon as possible, but it won't do me any good if I don't know what they look like."

"I really don't see your concern with this affair, Mr. Adams—"

Clint reached across the desk and plucked the man's glasses from his nose. The little man reacted as if Clint had struck him, rearing back in his chair.

"Really, I see no need for violence, Mr. Adams—"

"If you think that was violent, Mr. Wolf, wait until

you see what I'm going to do next."

"Milly was here yesterday!" the bank manager said, hurriedly. "I will have her describe the men to you."

"Fine. I'll just go and get her."

Clint went to the door, opened it, and called Milly into the office.

"I have a customer—" she started to say, but Clint cut her off.

"This will only take a moment."

Milly apologized to the woman she had been servicing and entered the office. She regarded Wolf with her hands clasped behind her back.

"Milly, tell this man—"

"Adams," Clint said to her, "Clint Adams."

"Clint Adams!" Wolf said, but Clint ignored him and concentrated on the girl.

"All right, Milly. How many men came into the bank?"

"Three," she said. "Two others were outside by the door, and one was holding the horses."

"How did you see all that?"

"Through the window."

"Can you describe any of the men to me?"

"The three who entered the bank, I can."

"Fine," Clint said, "go ahead and do so."

"Well, two of them looked a lot alike. They were tall, with brown hair, both on the skinny side. I'd bet they were brothers."

"Any scars that you noticed? Or something about the way they moved or walked?"

"One of them—the one who stuck the gun through my cage—had a small scar on his chin, here," she said, touching her skin.

"What kind of scar?"

"Like he'd been in a fight once and somebody with

a ring had hit him and cut him."

"A crescent shape?"

"Exactly!"

"And was he one of the brothers?"

"Yes."

"What about the third man?"

"He was bigger, maybe a little older than the others. They were late twenties, early thirties. This one was in his forties. He had a long jaw and a cruel mouth, and he had something in his mouth."

"Like what?"

"Oh, a toothpick, or maybe a match stick."

"Who spoke to you?"

"The one with the scar spoke to me, but the older one called out to everyone to stay still. He's the one who said it was a holdup."

"All right, Milly," Clint said, "you can go back to work now. Thank you very much."

"Are you going after them, Mr. Adams?"

"Yes, Milly, I am."

"Well, good luck, then."

"Thank you, Milly."

After Milly left, Clint turned and looked at the bank manager, who was staring at him. Obviously, he had not known who Clint was until he had introduced himself to Milly by his first name.

"Uh, I hope that was helpful, Mr. Adams."

"It was very helpful, Mr. Wolf, and you've just been a peach."

"Well, I like to cooperate—"

"I could tell, Mr. Wolf," Clint handed Wolf back his glasses and said, "Good day."

Clint's next stop was the sheriff's office, where he went through the Wanted posters in the deceased lawman's desk. Milly's description had been quite good, especially the business about the scar, and the man with the long jaw. Before long, Clint had located both of them.

The man with the scar was Will Lanahan. Obviously, the man who looked like his brother *was* his brother, Len Lanahan.

The man with the long jaw could have been Sam Bigelow.

Clint took all three posters, folded them up and put them in his pocket. He then left the office and walked to Doc Prentiss's.

"There was no change overnight, Mr. Adams," Prentiss told him.

"Does that mean he didn't get any worse?"

"No worse, and no better."

"Are you equipped to keep him here, Doc?"

"Where would you move him to?"

"His own room, over the saloon."

"No, I'll keep him here," Prentiss said, after a moment's thought. "The move might cause the bullet in his chest to shift."

"All right then," Clint said. "I'll be leaving town today—"

"Going where?"

"After the men who robbed the bank, killed two lawmen, and shot Rick."

"Well, I hope you catch them."

"I hope so, too, Doc," Clint said. "At least I know who I'm looking for. That's half the battle, right there."

"It's the other half that could kill you."

"I'm aware of that, Doctor. Uh, can I see Rick before I leave?"

"Why?"

Clint shrugged.

"Maybe just to satisfy myself that he's still breathing."

The doctor thought a moment, then said, "I don't see why not. Come with me."

Doc Prentiss led Clint to another room, where Rick was lying on a table. There were some belts around his waist, chest and wrists, probably to keep him from falling off the table and killing himself.

"Don't stay long," Prentiss said, and left Clint alone with Rick.

Clint looked down at his friend and felt the bile rise in his throat. His face was bruised and puffed, almost beyond recognition, and his color was so pale that he was almost paper-white. He was breathing, though. Clint watched the slow rhythm of it for a few moments, then touched his friend's hand.

"It doesn't mean much to you now, Rick, but I'll get the bastards. I'll get them."

When he left he didn't stop to talk to Prentiss. He didn't want the man to see the tears that were stinging his eyes.

"I still think that you should let me go with you," T.C. said while Clint finished saddling Duke.

"You'll do more good here, T.C. How are the girls holding up?"

"Just fine. Gloria's got them in high spirits, even."

"When I come back," Clint said, swinging into the saddle, "I'll have to make sure I get to know Gloria."

"I think you'd both like that," T.C. said with a grin. "I think you'd both like that a whole lot."

"Do me a favor while I'm gone, T.C.," Clint said.

"What's that?"

It was unfair, Clint knew, but he said, "Don't let him die."

SIX

The trail was cold.

He knew it would be when he left Labyrinth, but that didn't matter all that much. He figured that after hitting a bank and killing two lawmen, the only logical place for them to go was Mexico, even before they split the money.

Clint simply rode south, bypassing small towns and stopping at the larger ones. It wasn't until he reached a town called Palmersville that he found out he was on the right trail.

Clint hadn't been in Palmersville for a long time. The last time he'd been there the saloon had a bartender named Bill Chambers. He wondered if the man still worked there.

He left his horse at the livery and walked to the saloon. When he entered, he saw Bill Chambers behind the bar. A man of medium height, Chambers was stocky and powerfully built and ruggedly good-looking. He'd aged some since the last time Clint had seen him—but hadn't everyone?[1]

"How about some service here?" Clint called out.

Chambers, who had been deep in conversation, looked

---

[1] *THE GUNSMITH #7: THE LONGHORN WAR*

over, his annoyance plain on his face, but it quickly changed to a look of pleasure when he saw Clint Adams.

"Clint, you old son of a gun!"

He hurried down the bar and shook hands vigorously.

"What are you doing around here? It's been years."

"It has been that, Bill."

"Got some gray hairs, I see," Chambers said.

"They match yours."

"Yeah, we're getting old, all right. What can I get you?"

"Beer, a nice cold one."

"Coming up."

When Chambers returned, he placed a frosty mug in front of Clint and watched with pleasure as Clint drained half of it.

"Been riding long?" Chambers asked.

"I have, Bill. I'm hunting some men."

"Who?"

"The Lanahan brothers and a man named Sam Bigelow."

"Don't know the names," Chambers said. "Any descriptions?"

"Better than that," Clint said, and took out the posters.

Chambers smoothed them out on the bartop and studied them.

"I've seen these fellas."

"You have?" Clint said, becoming instantly alert. "When?"

"Couple of days ago, I think. They were in here, had a few drinks, didn't cause any trouble, and then left."

"How many men with them?"

"Two more."

"Only two?"

"That's it. Five in all. How many men you trailing?"

"Six, I thought."

"What'd they do?"

"Held up a bank in Labyrinth, killed the sheriff and his deputy, and seriously injured a friend of mine."

"Sorry to hear it. I hope your friend will be all right."

"So do I," Clint said. "Well, Bill, it was good to see you. I wasn't sure you'd still be working here."

"Working here, hell," Chambers said, "I own the place now."

"Good for you!" Clint said. "A businessman, huh?"

"That's me. It was good to see you, too, Clint. Stop in on your way back and stay longer."

"I just might do that," Clint said. "So long, Bill."

Any thought of possibly staying in town even an hour longer was gone. He knew he was two days behind them, so it was no time to be taking a rest.

"What's wrong with Kyle?" Sam Bigelow asked Len.

Len turned in his saddle to look at his younger brother, who was lagging behind.

"He's been feeling guilty ever since Hall died."

"Feel's responsible, I guess."

"I guess so."

"You can't see it, huh?" Bigelow asked.

"Nobody gets someone else killed, Sam," Len said. "Kyle didn't force Randy Hall to stand outside that bank."

"Maybe not, but right now I guess your little brother feels like he's killed his first man. He'll get over it soon enough."

"Sure he will," Len Lanahan said, "as soon as he kills one for real."

SEVEN

Palmersville was right across the Rio Grande from Mexico, so Clint was able to camp for the night in the foreign country that he found so beautiful under normal circumstances.

Now he had little time to notice the beauty of Mexico when he was chasing five men—or was it six?—who might just have killed one of his best friends. For all he knew, while he was sitting around his fire, being careful not to stare into it and destroy his night vision—Rick Hartman could have been dying . . . or already dead.

Clint had lost friends to violence before, the most prominent example of that being Wild Bill Hickok, who was shot from behind by a coward. When that happened it had brought home to Clint Adams—the famous Gunsmith!—his own mortality, and he took refuge inside of a bottle. It was Rick Hartman who'd pulled him out of that bottle, and since then they'd become very close friends.

Now he was in danger of losing Hartman to a violent death, and he was angry at the men who had done this to his friend.

When he found them he wanted to kill them.

Whether or not he *would* kill them was something he would have to deal with when the time came.

All he knew now was that he wanted to.

It was not a feeling he was enjoying.

In the morning he made a pot of coffee and took the time to drink it. He did not make anything to eat. In fact, he hadn't been eating much since he'd taken to the trail on this . . . this hunt. His stomach rebelled every time he thought about putting food into it. He didn't think he'd be able to eat until he caught the men he was after, and until Rick Hartman recovered—or died.

Saddling Duke, he wondered what would have happened if he hadn't met Marcy in Mercer, if he'd arrived in Labyrinth a day early. He would have been there to help Rick, and to help the sheriff and his deputy against the bank robbers.

Would it have made a difference? Well, he'd learned a long time ago that his presence with a gun often made a difference. He used to complain a lot about his reputation, but he'd come to terms with it of late. He was only sorry it had taken him so many years to do it.

Now he was sorry that he hadn't been in Labyrinth that morning, with a gun in his hand.

Maybe Rick wouldn't be in imminent danger of dying.

Maybe two lawmen wouldn't be dead.

Maybe he wouldn't be in Mexico, trailing five or six men, with intentions of killing them.

Mounting up and starting off, he was thinking that maybe he was giving himself too much goddamned credit.

At least, he hoped so.

EIGHT

"All right," Yates said, "we're in Mexico. Let's divvy up the money."

"You're an impatient man, Yates."

"When it comes to money, I am," Yates said to Will Lanahan. "My money, that is."

Will looked at Len, who said, "Yeah, it's time to split it up."

They were in a town called Santa Flores, which was little more than a collection of adobe walls, some of which even got together to form buildings. They were in one of the buildings, which was supposed to be a cantina.

"Get some beer, kid," Len said to Kyle.

"Sure . . ." the kid said distractedly. He still hadn't recovered from the death of his friend.

"Sam, the door," Len said. "We don't want some peasant walking in while we got the money on the table."

"Right."

"Will, you and me will count."

"Hey," Yates said, "I wanna count, too."

"I'd love to have you count, Yates," Len said, "but we got more than ten dollars here, and I've never known you to be able to count that high."

"Very—"

"Are you telling me you don't trust me and my brother, Yates?" Len asked. His gaze was cold, and Yates backed away from it a few steps.

"Naw, I ain't sayin' that, Len."

"Then shut up and let us count."

"Sure, Len, sure," Yates said. As Kyle came over carrying two mugs of beer for his brothers Yates took one from him.

"Hey—"

"Get some more, kid," Yates said.

Kyle set the one remaining beer down on the table where his brothers were sitting, and then went back to the bar to get another from the sleepy-eyed Mexican bartender.

"You got any women around here?" he asked the man.

"Women?" the men replied. "*Sí, señor,* we have women, but they usually like to meet men, *comprendé*?"

The bartender was a hulking, florid-faced man with a big belly and a full beard. He was grinning at Kyle now, revealing gaps where there used to be teeth.

"You *comprendé* this, friend," Kyle said, trying to sound like Len. "My brothers and I are gonna want some company tonight, and you're gonna provide it. Three señoritas . . . *comprendé*?"

The man's grin slipped and he said, "*Sí, señor, tres señoritas.*"

"Let me have two more beers."

The man nodded and drew two more beers for Kyle Lenahan, who was feeling his oats at the moment.

Kyle took the two beers back to the table and put one down for his brothers. As he was about to drink the other one, Sam Bigelow's big hand took it away from him.

"Thanks, kid."

"Shit!" Kyle said, and went back to the bar.

"All right," Len said, and Yates moved closer to the

table. "We got us thirty-four thousand dollars."

"That's all?" Yates asked.

"Hey, that's a good haul, Yates," Len said, "except to somebody as greedy as you."

"All right, all right. How much does my share come to?"

"Sixty-eight hundred."

"I risked my neck for less than seven thousand dollars?"

"Sounds good to me," Sam Bigelow said from the door.

"Me, too," Will said.

Yates blew air out from between his lips in disgust and said, "All right, let me have it."

"You figured wrong, Len," Kyle said, coming over to the table with his own beer.

"What are you talking about, kid?" Yates said.

"Your share comes to five thousand six hundred and sixty-six dollars and sixty cents, Yates."

"What the hell are you talking about?" Yates demanded.

"Back off, Yates," Len said coldly. He looked at his younger brother and said, "What *are* you talking about, kid?"

"Randy."

Len and Will Lanahan exchanged glances.

"Randy's dead, Kyle," Len said.

"So what? He's still got a share coming."

"How do you figure—" Yates snapped.

"He was part of this gang!"

"This ain't no gang, kid," Yates said. "We got together for this one job, and we only split with the survivors."

"That's bullshit, Yates," Kyle said. "Besides, you aren't the one who says how we split. Len decides that."

Kyle looked at his brother Len, waiting for his decision.

Len looked down at the money and counted out the shares. He picked one stack up and handed it to Yates.

"What's this?" Yates demanded.

"Your share."

Yates riffled through it and knew it was short of sixty-eight hundred—way short.

"You're kidding," Yates said. "You're going along with the kid?"

"With my brother, Yates."

"No way," Yates said angrily. "Lanahan, you can't—"

"Shut up, Yates!" Len Lanahan said. "Now either you take your share and get out, or you'll get nothing."

"Lanahan—"

"I mean it!"

Len Lanahan hadn't even bothered to stand up from his chair, but he was still getting the best of Yates in a classic staredown.

Finally Yates turned on his heel and stalked past Sam Bigelow, out of the cantina.

"I'll make sure he gets on his way," Sam Bigelow said, and followed Yates out.

"Okay," Len said to Kyle, setting a stack of bills aside, "what do you expect to do with Randy's share?"

Kyle picked up the stack and then tossed it back into the center of the table.

"Figure it in, brother," Kyle said. "This gives us over seven thousand each—including Sam, of course."

Len looked at Will, who was staring at Kyle with his mouth open.

"You're learning, kid," Len Lanahan said to his little brother, "you're finally learning."

NINE

Clint Adams rode into Little Mesa, wondering if Duke was as tired as he was. Now, that was stupid! Duke had been carrying *him* all this time, not the other way around. Of course the big gelding was tired.

Clint found the livery in the small town and told the liveryman that he would take care of his horse himself.

Then he took the saddle off the big gelding and cooled him down and fed him and apologized to him.

"I'm sorry, big boy," he said, slapping the big horse's rump. "I've been pushing so hard I never gave a thought to you. Well, tonight you rest."

Duke's big head bobbed up and down and Clint decided to take that as a thank-you.

"You're welcome," he said, and left to find himself a bed to rest in.

It had been a week since he'd left Palmersville. At that point he'd been two days behind them, at least. Was he still two days behind? As hard as he was pushing, had he fallen farther behind them?

Was he even going in the right direction anymore?

Yeah, he was on the right track. He could feel it. He just had to keep at it.

Just keep at it.

• • •

Win Yates looked down at the top of the head of the girl who was working on him with her mouth. These Mex women, they were hot for *gringo* men—especially *gringo* men with money. Yates may not have gotten as much as he would have liked from that Texas bank job—and he knew those Lanahan brothers had robbed him—but he still had a poke of five thousand dollars. That was enough to get this Mex gal to give him the best frenching he ever had.

This wasn't the first gal he'd tried, either. He'd been spreading his money around town since he arrived. Women, food, booze, gambling, and he still had five thousand left.

"Mmmm," the girl moaned around his swollen penis.

"You like that, huh, little bitch?" he asked.

"Oh, *señor*," she said, releasing him, "it is *magnifico!*"

"Sure it is," he said to her. "Well, come on girl, finish me. Finish me good!"

Clint got himself a room at the small hotel and then found his weary way to the cantina.

"*Cerveza,*" he ordered.

When the bartender brought the beer Clint asked, "Can I get any food?"

"Tacos?" the man asked.

"That's fine."

"You wait at a table."

Clint turned and saw that there were four tables in the place, none of them taken. In fact, he was the only person in the place.

He picked a table and sat down. Before long, a young woman with long black hair, dark skin, dark eyebrows, and a lowcut peasant blouse that showed off a full bosom came out carrying a plate.

"Tacos?" she asked.

Since he was the only guy in the place he thought it was a silly question, but he said, "Yeah, tacos."

She put the plate down in front of him.

"I hope it is enough," she said.

He looked at the four tacos on the plate and said, "It should be plenty. Thank you."

"My name is Angela."

"Clint," he said. "I'm glad to meet you, Angela."

"Enjoy the tacos, Clint. If I can get you anything else, let me know."

"This'll be fine."

"If you want to gamble there is a larger cantina—"

"This one is fine, Angela. Thank you."

As it turned out it was more than just fine. The food was good, the beer was cold . . . and Angela went back to his room with him.

Clint didn't have any illusions about why Angela went to his room with him. She was a pretty girl in a small town looking for a way out. He knew why he had taken her back to his room, and he hadn't been disappointed. She was energetic and eager, and she had a lush, young body that he explored with his hands and his mouth.

When they were finished she snuggled up to him as he drifted along half asleep, half awake.

"So," she said, "you do not want to impress all the young *señoritas* in Mexico with your money and your manhood?"

"What money?" he asked, sleepily.

"Well," she said, sliding her hand down between his

legs, "you have the manhood."

"Yeah . . ." he said, smiling as she manipulated him. "You're beating a dead horse there, Angela. I'm finished for the night."

"I do not think so," she said, moving down between his legs.

She used her mouth and tongue to bring him erect again and then climbed atop him. He reached for her breasts while she rode him, tweaking the nipples between his fingers, and then bringing her down to his mouth so he could bite and suck them.

"Mmm," she said, "the other girls say that the other *gringo* in town has a lot of money but you have . . . have . . . ooh, *Dios mio*!!"

"Angela . . ."

"Hmm?"

"Angela, are you awake?"

"Mmm . . ."

"Something you said earlier," Clint said, touching her shoulder.

"Hmm? What did I say?"

"About another *gringo* with a lot of money."

"Hmm."

"Have you see him? Have you been with him?"

"I have seen him . . ." she said sleepily, ". . . but I have not been with him. I do not go with a man for money."

"Where is this man, Angela? Where?"

"Here, in the hotel."

"And how much money do they say he has?"

She was more awake now.

"A lot, a lot of American money, and he is spending it . . ."

"A lot of money," Clint said. He looked down at Angela and said, "Go to sleep, Angela. Go to sleep."

"Mmm," she said, and snuggled up against him.

A lot of money, she'd said.

How much, he wondered, was a lot of money to the people of Little Mesa?

TEN

Clint woke in the morning with something tickling his nose. He reached up to push it away and Angela squealed. His fingers came away moist.

He opened his eyes and found her crouched over him, her womanhood inches from his face. She had been tickling his nose with her pubic hair.

He picked up his head and stuck out his tongue. He licked her, enjoying the sharp taste of her, and then found her clit, straining and ready. He worked on her just that way until she came, her legs shuddering, and she fell across his chest.

"Now that's what I call a wake-up call," he said.

"*Dios*," she said, "it is what I call . . . ah, there are no words."

"That's okay," he said, flipping her over onto her back, "I don't want to talk, anyway."

"There is another *gringo* in town," Clint said to the desk clerk. His name was Arturo, and he was looking at the money Clint had put on the desk in front of him.

"*Sí, señor.*"

"And he has a room here."

"*Sí, señor.*"

"What room is he in?"

"*Numero cinco, señor,*" the man said.

"In English," Clint said, even though he was sure he understood.

"Room five, *señor.*"

Room five was down the hall from his own room, which was eight. In the whole hotel, there were only eight rooms.

"Is he still up there?" Clint asked.

The man nodded, still eyeing the money greedily.

"Is anyone with him?"

"Carmen Sanchez," Arturo said.

"Who is she?"

The man shrugged and said, "*A puta, señor*—just a whore."

"How is he registered?"

"As Yates, *señor.*"

"Fine," Clint said. He picked his hand up, releasing the money, and the man snatched it up.

Angela had left and it was still early—early enough for the other *gringo* in town to still be in his room.

Clint went to room five and put his ear to the door. The noises inside sounded like the noise he and Angela had been making less than half an hour ago. He knocked. If he was wrong about the man, he'd apologize.

If he was right he'd do a lot more.

He waited a moment then knocked again.

"Go away!"

"This is important!"

There was some muffled conversation on the other end and then a man's voice said, "So is this."

Clint stepped back, then kicked out once. The door was so flimsy it sprang open, almost falling off its hinges. He stepped quickly into the room, gun drawn.

On the bed a man and woman were both naked, the man atop her. As the man looked over his shoulder Clint found himself looking at both the man's face and his ass.

"What the fuck—" the man said.

"Get up."

"What's going on—"

"Just get off the bed!"

The man obeyed and stood there naked and vulnerable. His penis, which had very recently been hard at work inside the girl, had now shriveled comically.

"Look, if this is a holdup I don't have much money," the man said.

"That's not what I've heard all over town," Clint said.

The woman on the bed was watching the gun carefully, but was making no attempt to cover her nakedness. She had a nice body, but nowhere as good as Angela's, nor was she as young.

"Relax, lady," Clint said.

"All right, so I've got some money," Yates said. "I'll give it to you."

"How much?"

"What?"

"How much do you have?"

Yates hesitated, then shrugged and said, "A few hundred, I guess."

"A few hundred."

"Yeah. I drove a herd to Texas, then came over here to spend my pay."

"And you've got a few hundred."

"Honest, mister, that's all."

"You've never driven cattle a day in your life," Clint said, "and you probably haven't drawn an honest breath, either."

"Hey, look—" Yates said, but he stopped when Clint lifted his gun.

"Just stand still while I look in your saddlebags," Clint said.

"My saddle—hey, look, I'll get the money for you, friend—"

"I'll get it myself, if you don't mind—even if you do."

Clint moved across the room to a hard-backed chair, where the saddlebags were resting. Keeping an eye on Yates, he groped into the saddlebag and when he withdrew his hand was holding a wad of money.

"Looks like more than a few hundred here, Yates," he said. "Where did you get it?"

"A poker game," Yates said, "I won it in a poker game."

"In this town?"

"Uh, well, no—I mean, I won it in a few poker games."

"You must be a real good poker player, huh, Yates?"

"Fair," Yates said, "I get lucky."

"Well, your luck just ran out."

"Whattaya mean?"

"I mean that if you lie to me again I'm going to shoot off your balls."

"What?" Yates looked like he was in shock and in pain just from the thought of such a thing.

"You heard me."

"Mister, I don't know what you want, but—"

"I want the truth," Clint said. "Where did you get that money?"

"I told you, I won it—"

"That's a lie," Clint said, cocking his gun. "Say good-bye to your left ball."

"Wait! Jesus, gimme a chance!"

Yates was sweating and the smell of it filled the room. It was not pleasant, but then the smell of fear never is.

"To think up a new lie?" Clint said, shaking his head. "Not very likely, Yates. Now, where did you get all this money?"

"A bank," Yates said, "I got it from a bank."

"A bank that you robbed?"

"That's right."

"In Texas?"

"Yes."

"Where you killed a couple of lawmen?"

"Look," Yates said nervously, "what are you, a bounty hunter? I've got more money in that saddlebag than I do on my head. Take it!"

"I don't want the money."

"What do you want?" Yates cried out in fear.

"I want you to tell me about the bank job, Yates. I want you to tell me who shot the sheriff, who shot the deputy, and then who shot the man in the street with the shotgun. And then I want you to tell me where I can find all of these people."

"All right, all right," Yates said. "I'll tell you what I know."

"Make it good, Yates," Clint warned, "because if I don't believe you—if I doubt one word of your story—I'm still going to shoot off your balls."

ELEVEN

"All right," Yates said, "just take it easy with that gun."

"You worry about what you're going to tell me," Clint said, "and I'll worry about the gun. Okay? Talk to me."

"Listen," the girl on the bed said, "if you fellas are gonna talk, I gotta go someplace."

"Where?" Clint asked.

"I gotta make a living, you know."

"All right," Clint said. "Get dressed and go."

The girl got up and got dressed while Clint watched Yates and Yates watched Clint's gun.

"You two don't do much for a girl's ego, do you?" she complained.

"I'm sorry," Clint said. "You're very pretty."

"He owes me money," she said.

"Take what he owes you out of the saddlebag."

The girl went to the saddlebag and started leafing through the bills.

"Take just what he owes you," Clint said.

The girl gave him a look, then took one of the bills and straightened up.

"Have fun, boys."

She left, pulling the door closed behind her. Clint

turned his head for a split second, to make sure the door *did* close, and then looked back at Yates.

"Now that we're alone—"

Clint didn't know where the gun came from but suddenly it was in Yates' hand. It must have been underneath the sheet on the bed.

Yates was bringing the gun to bear on Clint and the Gunsmith reacted by pure reflex. He pulled the trigger and his bullet punched a hole in Yates' chest. The man staggered back and fell to the floor. His foot tangled in the sheet and pulled it off the bed, where it covered half of him—the top half. As Clint watched, the man's blood began to soak through the sheet.

"Shit!" he said, and holstered his gun.

He was in the lobby when the town sheriff ambled in, looking unconcerned.

"I heard a shot," he said to the clerk.

The clerk inclined his head in Clint's direction. The lawman looked over at Clint and then approached him.

"I am *El Jefe*," he said, proudly.

The man was about thirty and already beginning to show a large gut from too much beer and food—probably all free.

"Good for you."

"I heard a shot," the man went on. "It is my job to look into such things."

"Upstairs you'll find a dead man," Clint said. "In the room with him you'll find a saddlebag full of money. The money is from a bank robbery that was committed in Labyrinth, Texas."

"I am not concerned with a robbery committed in Texas—"

"He and some friends of his killed the sheriff and his

deputy, shot a friend of mine and left him for dead."

"And you have had your revenge on him," the sheriff said. "Well, that is fine with me."

"No, you've got it wrong," Clint said. "I didn't intend to kill him."

"It is all right," the sheriff assured him. "I am not going to arrest you. You've avenged your friend, and the lawman— "

"You're not listening," Clint said, cutting the man off. "I wanted him alive so he could tell me where the others have gone."

"Then why is he dead?"

"He pulled a gun on me!"

The sheriff shrugged and said, "Fine."

The man still believed that Clint had killed Yates out of a thirst for revenge, and he didn't seem to be able to change the man's mind.

"Forget it," Clint said. "The body's all yours, sheriff. I'll be taking the money back to Texas."

"That is fine with me."

Clint stared at the man and said, "I *will* be returning the money to Texas."

"Of course you will," the sheriff said.

"Shit," Clint said, and left the lobby.

Clint left Duke in front of the sheriff's office and entered.

"Ah, *Señor* Adams," the sheriff said, standing up. He looked nervous, and since he called Clint by name it was safe to assume he knew who Clint was. "I have the money ready for you."

"Good," Clint said. He moved forward and accepted Yates' saddlebags from the lawman. "Thanks."

"It is my pleasure to serve you, *señor*," the sheriff

said. "Earlier, I did not know who you were—"

"Is that important?"

"Even here we have heard of the famous Gunsmith, *señor*," the man said.

"Yeah," Clint said. He tossed the saddlebags over his shoulder and left.

Outside he secured the saddlebags to his saddle and mounted up.

He'd found one of them but now he was back where he started. All he knew now was that they had divided the money and had possibly split up.

It was going to take him even longer if he had to hunt them down one by one.

TWELVE

Clint dragged his ass into Madera five days later, no closer to finding the remaining men than he had been five days earlier, when he'd shot Yates. It seemed as if his luck had turned bad as soon as he pulled the trigger on the man.

He dismounted in front of the livery, wondering what the odds were against his coincidentally running into one of the other men the way he had stumbled onto Yates. *That* had been his chance, and he'd ruined it by killing the man. He couldn't very well expect another opportunity like that to fall into his lap . . . could he?

Maybe if he stayed in Mexico long enough, and went to enough towns . . .

Ah, by now one or more of them could have been back in the United States.

He left Duke in the care of the appreciative liveryman and went to the nearest cantina for a beer. He took the brew to a table and sat alone with his thoughts.

If the Lanahan brothers and Sam Bigelow were the only ones left, it stood to the reason that at least the three brothers would stay together. Bigelow might have gone his own way, but the brothers would stay together. How difficult would it be for three brothers with reputations to keep out of trouble in Mexico? Sooner or later some word of their whereabouts would have to get out. The question was, should he stay in one place and wait for that to happen or keep moving?

Staring into his beer, he wondered how Rick was doing. He decided that the next town he stopped in would have to have a telegraph wire so he could check on Rick's condition.

He finished the beer and took the empty mug back to the bar.

"*Uno mas, señor?*" the bartender asked.

"No, not right now, thanks," Clint said. "How many hotels does this town have?"

"One."

"That's what I figured," Clint said. "I'll probably be back later for another beer."

"*Bien, señor.*"

Clint left and found the hotel. Madera was a fair-sized town as far as sleepy Mexican towns went, and the hotel actually had two floors. It was also—according to the register Clint signed—mostly empty.

"Are there any other *gringos* in the hotel?" he asked the young man behind the desk.

"No, *señor*," the man said. "No others."

"Thanks."

Clint went up to his room, tossed his saddlebags on a chair, and laid down on the bed fully dressed. In a matter of moments, he was alseep.

Clint came awake with a start, angry at himself for falling asleep, but it was just further indication that he had been pushing himself too hard. Maybe he should be satisfied with the one man he'd managed to track down— or trip over—and the money he'd recovered.

He used the pitcher and basin on the rickety dresser

to wash himself awake, and then left to go back to the cantina.

"Ready for that beer, *señor*?" the bartender asked.

"I guess so."

The bartender set it on the bar while Clint looked the place over. When he'd been there earlier he'd been the only customer. Now there were several men seated at tables, and two standing at the bar. There was a young woman working the tables, but Clint didn't think she was a pro. She was simply ferrying drinks back and forth from the bar to the tables. One of the men, however, took that moment to decide that he wanted a little more than that from her.

"Hey, *chica*," he said, grabbing her ass with one big hand.

"No!" she said, flinching from his touch, but he managed to snake his arm around her waist and pull her onto his lap.

"Stop," she said, "No, *por favor*."

The man said something to her in Spanish that Clint didn't understand and grabbed one of her breasts, squeezing it brutally. The girl cried out in pain.

"Who is she?" he asked the bartender.

"My sister," he said, looking unconcerned.

"And you're letting that go on?"

"He's just playing with her," the bartender said. "Besides, she's got to learn how to handle men like that."

"How old is she?"

"Sixteen."

"Maybe it's too early for her to start those lessons."

"Not in Mexico."

No, Clint thought, not even the United States, for that matter, but there was something about the way the man was manhandling the girl that he didn't like.

He put the beer mug down on the bar and walked over to the table where the girl was still writhing in the man's lap, trying to get away.

"Excuse me," Clint said. He grabbed the girl's arm and pulled her from the man's lap.

"Hey!" the man said, glaring at Clint.

The girl instinctively moved behind Clint.

"What?" Clint asked, looking down at the man.

The man frowned for a moment, then made what for him seemed to be a very difficult decision.

He stood up, towering over Clint.

"That's my woman."

"Is she? Why don't we ask her?"

Clint looked over his shoulder and said, "Are you his woman?"

"No!" the girl spat. She peeked out at the man, then ducked back behind Clint.

"She says she's not your woman."

"What she says doesn't matter, *señor*," the big man replied.

"Why not?"

The man frowned again. It seemed that the mere act of thought was a chore for him.

"Uh . . ."

"She's a child, friend," Clint said, putting his hand on the man's shoulder. "Why not let her be and find yourself a woman."

Now, thinking gave the man a problem, but action he knew very well, and he construed Clint's hand on his shoulder as an action taken against him.

That could only be met one way.

His right fist came up and impacted against Clint's jaw. Clint was driven backward, pushing the young girl along with him. He staggered, not wanting to fall on her, but he was not able to retain his feet. He went down, and she went down beneath him.

He rolled off of her immediately and turned, still on the floor.

"Are you all right?" he asked, with concern.

She smiled at him and said, "I am not hurt."

He stood up, then reached down to assist her to her feet.

"Look out!" she shouted, pushing herself back against the base of the bar.

Clint turned his head in time to catch the big man's fist in the jaw again. He went down again, onto all fours. Without time to think he reacted by instinct. Expecting the man to kick him he reached out to intercept and was rewarded when the man's boot landed in his grasp. He twisted and pushed upward, and the big Mexican went over backward.

He stood up as the man crashed onto a table, splintering it and taking the pieces to the floor with him. He helped the girl to her feet and then looked at the bartender.

"Who is this man?"

"His name is Ramon Ortega," the bartender said. "He kills people with his bare hands."

Clint looked at Ortega, who was lumbering to his feet and said, "Charming."

Ortega had righted himself and faced Clint with his massive fists clenched.

"All right, Ortega," Clint said. He felt something on his lip and touched it with his finger. It was blood. "You've had two shots at me. Let's call it even."

"You put your hand on me," Ortega said.

"And you've more than had your revenge," Clint said. "There's no need for anyone to get hurt."

"You are going to get hurt," Ortega said, "not me."

"There's no way for me to talk you out of this?" Clint asked.

"No!"

Clint could have drawn his gun and shot Ortega, but that wasn't his way. The man had made no move toward his own weapon, which was tucked into his belt.

"All right," Clint said, "discard your gun."

"Huh?"

"Put your gun aside," Clint said, "and I'll put mine aside. You want to settle this with your hands, don't you?"

"Oh yes."

Ortega pulled his gun from his belt and handed it to a friend.

As Clint unbuckled his gunbelt, the bartender said softly, "Your best bet is to shoot him where he stands . . . now!"

"That's not the way I work," Clint said. He handed the bartender his gunbelt.

"Then this is the way you will die," the man said.

"He will not die," the girl said. Clint didn't see the adoring look in her eyes as she looked at him.

"Let's hope nobody does," Clint said.

"Ah," the bartender said, "but to beat Ortega, you'll have to kill him."

"All right, *gringo*," Ortega said. "Now you will die!"

Clint looked at the girl and said, "Everybody seems to have that opinion except you."

"I am Lisa."

"Glad to meet you," Clint said, and turned to meet Ortega's charge.

As the man rushed at him, Clint curled his foot around a nearby spittoon and kicked it into the man's path. Ortega flinched and slowed, and when the spittoon struck his foot it careened away, spilling its contents on the floor.

Clint leaped forward as the man slowed, and swung at him. His fist struck the man's chin, which felt as if it were made of rock. Ortega staggered, but shook the blow off. He swung at Clint, who ducked under it and hit Ortega in the gut. The big Mexican grunted, but the blow had no lasting effect. Ortega brought his hand down like a hammer on Clint's back. Clint gasped and spun away, eluding a second blow.

They faced each other now, measuring, weighing. Clint decided that his patience was his best weapon against a man who was used to doing his thinking with his fists.

He waited.

"Come," Ortega said, "fight me."

"I am."

"You're just standing there."

"So, come and get me."

"I will come and kill you."

As the big man started forward, Clint shifted his weight and kicked out. The toe of his boot struck Ortega's knee and the big Mexican screamed in pain. The leg buckled and he went down onto his good knee. From that position he was vulnerable, but Clint hesitated, unwilling to strike a helpless man. Still, he knew that if the tables were turned Ortega would have no compunction about striking him—and he would try as soon as the pain subsided and he was able to stand again.

Clint stepped forward and kicked Ortega in the head. The big Mexican tottered for a moment, then fell over onto his side, unconscious.

"You killed him," the bartender said.

"No," Clint said.

"Then you had better."

"No," Clint said again. He put his hand out for his gunbelt and when the bartender laid it in his palm he turned and left the cantina.

THIRTEEN

Clint went back to his hotel room and checked his cut lip in the dirty mirror. It wasn't badly cut, and the blood had already dried. He took off his shirt and washed his hands, face, and torso.

He knew he was lucky to have survived the fight with Ramon Ortega. If the man had been just a little smarter, things might have turned out differently.

In fact, if Clint had been a bit smarter it would have turned out differently. All he had to do was ignore what Ortega was doing to the girl. After all, her own brother wasn't concerned.

He dried his face and then shook his head at himself in the mirror. If he *had* ignored what was going on, he wouldn't be able to look himself in the mirror right now. It was worth a swollen lip to be able to do that.

He walked over to the bed and sat down on it. The mattress was so thin he could feel the springs beneath it.

He was about to recline on the bed when there was a knock on his door. He wondered if when he woke up Ortega would be angry enough to come to his hotel looking for him. He picked up his gun and took it to the door with him.

"Who is it?"

"It is Lisa."

He recognized her voice, but that didn't mean she was alone.

"What do you want?"

"I have brought you something."

"What?"

"Open the door, please, *señor*."

The tone was plaintive, and he unlocked the door and opened it. She was standing in the hall holding a covered plate of something that smelled good.

"I brought you dinner," she said.

"Dinner?"

"You have not had dinner yet, have you?" she asked, hopefully.

"Uh, no, I haven't," he said. He hadn't even thought about dinner. "Come in."

"*Gracias*," she said, entering. He closed the door and turned to face her.

"What did you bring me, Lisa?"

"Enchiladas," she said, removing the towel that was covering the food. "I made them myself."

She hadn't had time to cook anything since he'd left the cantina so he was fairly certain that if she had cooked them, it had been done earlier in the day and she had simply warmed them up for him. Still, they looked good and the smell was making him aware of the fact that he was hungry.

She had thought to bring utensils and now said, "Here, you eat. I will watch."

"All right," he said. He holstered his gun and left it hanging on the bedpost, within easy reach. He took the tray from her, set it on his lap, and began to eat. They were lukewarm after her walk over here, but he ate both of them with relish, wishing she'd thought to bring something to drink.

She watched him solemnly while he ate and when he was finished, she smiled and asked, "Did you like them?"

"They were delicious, Lisa," he said. "Thank you very much for thinking of me."

"You thought of me in the cantina," she said. "Even my brother did not try to stop that pig Ortega from putting his hands on me. He was very angry when he woke up."

He knew she was speaking about Ortega.

"I'm sure he was."

"He will try to kill you next time he sees you."

"I'll be leaving early in the morning," he said. "Maybe he won't see me."

She took the tray off the bed and set it on the dresser. When she turned to face him she was unfastening her skirt.

"Lisa—"

She dropped the skirt to the floor and her hands went to her blouse.

"Now we make love—"

"Lisa," he said, standing. She pulled her blouse up over her head and her small breasts lifted and then fell as she dropped it to the floor. Her breasts may have been small, but they had large, dark brown nipples, and they were very round and firm-looking.

"You don't have to do this out of gratitude, Lisa," Clint said. In spite of the fact that he knew she was little more than a child he felt himself responding to her nakedness.

"It is not out of gratitude," she said. "It is from love."

"Now, Lisa—"

"You do not have to love me back, *señor*," she said. "I do not expect that."

She walked up to him so that she was standing very close, almost touching. She was short, perhaps just an inch or two over five feet. Her black hair was very long and lustrous and her face was very pretty—even more so when she smiled.

"It will be enough for me that you make love with me," she said, moving to put her arms around his neck.

"Lisa, wait—" he said, taking her by the wrists.

"You do not like me?" she asked.

"I like you very much," he said. "I think you are very beautiful—"

"Then we make love—"

"No," he said, pressing her hands together between his. "I mean, I would love to make love to you, but—"

"But what?"

"You—you're very young, Lisa."

"I am experienced," she said.

"How old are you? Sixteen?"

"Seventeen. I will be eighteen soon."

"Soon?" he asked. "How soon?"

She smiled sheepishly and said, "In eleven months."

"Lisa—"

She slid her hands from between his and put them on his chest. Slowly she unbuttoned his shirt.

"I am very good, *Señor* Clint," she said. She slid her hands inside his shirt, and her touch was warm and gentle. She found his nipples and rubbed them with her index fingers. She leaned in, spread his shirt open, and tongued his left nipple.

"I am *very* good," she said, "very experienced."

She pulled his shirt from his pants, then undid his belt buckle while licking his other nipple. He felt himself swell to bursting and when she had his pants undone she reached for him and closed her small hand over him.

"Oooh," she said, "you are very large, *muy grande!* I knew you would be."

"Lisa—" he said, but his voice was weak, as was his protest.

"Shh," she said, squeezing his penis. "You will see, I will make you feel *very* good."

She released him and used her hands to push his pants and underwear down. He had already removed his boots and he lifted first one foot then the other to allow her to slip the garments off. As she took his erection into her hands and began to lick the swollen head, he discarded his shirt. He reached for her head then as she opened her mouth and took him inside. She kept her right hand around his base and hefted his balls with the left. As her head bobbed back and forth and she moaned around his thick length he remembered thinking that she was very good, indeed . . . and then all other thought became lost in pleasure.

FOURTEEN

Clint woke the next morning with Lisa curled up next to him. In bed she had not seemed at all like a child, but like the experienced woman she had told him she was. Idly, he wondered if she would have been able to handle Ortega without his help, but that was hindsight. The simple fact of the matter was that if he had not stepped in when he did, then she would not have come to his room last night—and he wouldn't have wanted to give that up for anything.

She seemed to sense that he was awake and she moaned and stretched, displaying herself to him. Her breasts lifted tautly and he leaned over to kiss them, licking the nipples, which reacted immediately.

"You did not get enough last night, Clint?" she asked.

"How could any man get enough of you, Lisa?"

"Ah," she said, wrapping her arms around his neck, "you say sweet things, even in the morning."

She pulled him down to her and kissed him, pulling his tongue into her mouth and chewing it. He had learned during the night that she enjoyed perhaps more than anything deep kissing, and he certainly didn't mind obliging her. Even when she had been sitting astride him, sliding up and down the length of him, she had managed to lean over for a long and deep kiss.

After he had slid down between her legs to return the pleasure she had given him with her mouth, she kissed him that way, even though his face and mouth were wet from her.

She continued to kiss now, moaning and writhing against him. He slid his hand down over her belly, through the thick tangle of wiry pubic hair until he could insert one finger inside of her. When his fingers were slick from her, he found her clit and began to stroke it, moving it in circles. She lifted her hips and he felt her grow taut and then shudder as he brought her to orgasm that way, and still she kissed him.

When the tremors had past she released his mouth and breathed deeply.

"I will never meet another such as you," she said, and for a moment he was afraid that she was going to ask to go with him when he left.

"Lisa—"

"Oh, do not worry, Clint," she said, laughing, "I will not shame myself or make it difficult for you by asking to go with you. I know you are a man who must travel alone."

"If it was different, Lisa—"

"Shh," she said, pressing her index finger to his mouth. "*Por favor,* another kiss, this one for good-bye, no?"

"Yes," he said, "another kiss."

He kissed her and it was as if she wanted to devour him.

He did some devouring of his own . . .

He walked to the livery. The streets were empty and quiet—too quiet even for a sleepy town early in the morning. He wondered if they would wait until he reached the livery and try to get him when he rode out, or open fire before he reached the door. He would have to depend on his instincts to tell him when.

Clint Adams went into the livery and saddled Duke, while outside three men waited to kill him.

Ramon Ortega, a huge knot over his left eye where Clint Adams had kicked him, was across the street from the livery, behind a buckboard. He had been waiting there since first light, intent on taking his revenge against the man who had humiliated him.

On the roof of the livery itself was his *compadre*, Esteban Largo. Above him, on the roof of the Feed and Grain building, was his other partner, Jose Estrada.

Both Largo and Estrada kept their eyes on Ramon Ortega, for it would be at his word that they would fire at the *gringo*, killing him.

But first Ramon Ortega wanted to try him again—alone.

Clint walked Duke to the door of the livery and then stopped. He listened intently for a full minute, and then heard it again. The scrape of a booted foot on the roof as someone shifted position, probably looking for something a little more comfortable.

He put Duke in the first empty stall and walked to the front window. Looking outside he checked the rooftops across the street. Sure enough, up on top of the Feed & Grain he spotted another one. It was just the bob of a head as the second man also shifted, but it was enough to know that he was there. It was a sure thing that he wasn't up there repairing the roof.

Now he lowered his eyes and studied the street. There was a buckboard across the street that looked out of place. There was no team hitched to it, and yet it had been recently moved. The tracks in the street behind it attested to that fact.

He lowered his eyes even farther and looked underneath the buckboard at a man's legs. They were big legs, almost like tree trunks. It didn't take a genius to figure out who they belonged to.

He took a few moments to study the scene further, but three was all he saw.

Under any normal circumstances, three would have been more than enough.

FIFTEEN

Clint found a back way out of the livery and took it. There was a ladder built into the back wall of the livery and, from what he could see, it was the only way to the roof from the outside. There was bound to be a way from the inside, but he didn't have time to look for it.

He started up the ladder, hoping that the man on the roof would be looking the other way when he topped it.

When he reached the top rung he took off his hat and held it down by his side. He stuck his head up just enough to take a look. He saw the man's back as he was studying the street. How long would they wait, he wondered, before they figured something was wrong?

He was all the way at the back of the roof while the other man was standing at the front. Clint knew he'd never reach the man without being heard, and then he'd have to kill him, alerting the other two.

Clint ducked down and then rapped on the side of the building with his knuckles, as if he was knocking on a door. He waited a few seconds, then repeated the act, knocking again.

He waited, looking up above him, waiting for either the man's face or his gun to appear. Finally he heard a foot scrape the roof again, and then he saw the barrel of the man's gun clear the roof. He waited until the man's wrist was in view—just before the man's face would have appeared—and then reached up, grasped the wrist, and pulled.

Jose Estrada was so shocked at what had happened that he didn't make a sound as he flew over the roof's edge. In fact, he didn't make a sound until he hit the ground on his back. He grunted in pain, a sound that couldn't be heard out front, and then he sighed and passed out—or died, Clint didn't know which, and he wasn't that concerned. Still, when he got back to the ground he checked the man and found that he was still breathing. He'd either had the wind knocked out of him, or something was broken. The man would find out for himself when he woke up.

Now Clint knew he had two men to contend with, both out front. The rear door of the livery was only big enough for a man, not a horse, so there was no other way to get Duke out of the building except by the front door.

Well, there was no other way, then. He was going to have to go out the front and face them. His edge over them was that he knew there were more than one—and only he knew that now there were two of them, not three.

He entered the livery again and walked to the front. He retrieved Duke from the stall and walked to the door, trailing Duke behind him. He stepped outside and walked toward the center of the street.

At least he knew he wasn't going to be back-shot.

SIXTEEN

"Stand still, *gringo*," a man called out.

Clint recognized the voice as that of Ramon Ortega. No surprise there.

He stopped and stood still, but he released Duke's reins and the big gelding trotted off out of range.

"That you, Ortega?"

"It is me, *gringo*."

"You want to try me again?"

"You made a fool of me."

"You made a fool of yourself, Ramon," Clint said.

"I am going to kill you."

"Well then, step out here and have a go at it."

Ortega stepped out from behind the buckboard, which surprised Clint. He'd thought the man might try to shoot him from hiding.

Apparently, he had not given the man enough credit.

"How do we do it this time, Ramon?" Clint asked. "Fists, knives . . . guns?"

"Guns."

"Oh, Ramon," Clint said, "you're no gunman."

"Why do you say that?"

"Look at your hands," Clint said, and the man did just that. "They're full of knots, and your knuckles are all swollen. Your fingers are thick and stubby. Now look at mine."

Ortega looked up as Clint spread the fingers of his right hand.

"See, long and slim. Some might even call them graceful. These are the fingers of a man who knows how to use a gun."

Ortega stared at Clint's hand, and then down at his own. Clint risked a look up at the roof of the Feed and Grain and saw the second man looking down at him, gun in hand.

"Call your friend down from the roof, Ramon," Clint said. "There's no reason for anyone to get hurt."

Ramon looked up at Clint in surprise.

"Yeah, I know he's up there," Clint said, giving up his edge. It might have been a foolish move, but he thought there was a chance that he could talk Ortega out of this, and then he wouldn't have to kill him.

"I also know you had a man on the roof of the livery, only he's not there, anymore."

Ortega looked up at the roof of the livery.

"I'm going to get on my horse and ride out, Ramon," Clint said.

"You made a fool of me," Ortega said, licking his lips nervously.

"I told you, you did that yourself. If it hadn't been with me, it would have been with somebody else."

Ortega was unsure about what to do next. The man on the roof was getting nervous. If the big man didn't back down somebody was going to get hurt.

"All right, Ramon," Clint said, "either make a move for your gun or let me ride out. Which is it going to be?"

Ortega didn't answer.

Clint backed away and moved over toward Duke. The big gelding saw him coming and moved to meet him. Keeping his eye on Ortega, Clint mounted up. When he was astride Duke he looked at the man on the roof, who was as edgy as he was going to get.

Clint started to ride past Ortega. The big man frowning, still trying to decide what to do. The man on the roof was moving closer and closer to the edge, trying to keep Clint in sight. Finally, he moved a little too close and his foot slipped.

"Heyyy—" he shouted on his way down, his cry cut off when he hit the street.

Both Ortega and Clint looked down at him, and then the big Mexican looked at Clint.

"Forget it, Ramon," Clint said. "Just see to your friends. I'll be on my way and we'll never have to see each other again. How does that sound?"

Ortega thought a moment and then said, "That sounds fine, *señor*."

"I thought it might."

Clint left town then.

Time to get back to the business at hand.

SEVENTEEN

Len Lanahan took a table at the rear of the cantina, away from his brothers, who were bickering again. It seemed like all Will and Kyle did these days was argue. Len was sorry that Sam Bigelow had gone his own way. He got along better with Sam than he did with either of his brothers.

Sam and Len went back a long way, and when they split up after leaving a little town called Bonita, Sam had told Len to get in touch with him the next time he had a job . . .

"You're the first one I call, Sam," Len Lanahan told him. "You know that."

"Yeah, I know, Len," Sam had said.

Will and Kyle had ridden on ahead, and Sam jerked his head toward them.

"Don't let those two get you killed, Lenny," Bigelow said.

Len looked over at his brothers and said, "I promised Momma I'd watch over them."

"I know," Sam Bigelow said, "but don't forget to watch over yourself, huh?"

"I always do, Sam."

The two men shook hands then, and Bigelow rode off

in the opposite direction, heading back to Texas . . .

The Lanahan brothers had decided that not only would they stay in Mexico a little longer, but that they'd ride deeper still into Mexico until they found a town they liked enough to spend a couple of weeks in.

Actually, it was Len Lanahan who made all the decisions, and when they found the town called Angelina five days earlier he decided they'd stay awhile.

At first Will and Kyle had objected. They both wanted to go back to Texas. They weren't as patient as Len was—and they didn't know the value of waiting for the furor to die down after a murder and a bank robbery.

After Len had argued away their last objection, he had to deal with their objections to staying in Angelina. It was a small town with only a few buildings, one of which was the cantina, and another of which was the hotel. There was little else.

Of course, there was the girl named Lola, and that was now what Will and Kyle were arguing about.

"She wants a man, Kyle," Will said, "not a whelp like you."

"Let's go outside," Kyle said, "and I'll show you what a whelp I am."

Len studied the two men and decided that if he did let them go outside, he'd bet on Kyle. Their younger brother was coming along nicely into manhood while Will, although older, still had a lot of growing up to do and did more talking than anything else.

"I'm not gonna fight you, Kyle," Will said, "you're my baby brother."

"I'll show you who's a baby—"

"That's enough!" Len shouted.

Both brothers fell silent and looked at him.

RIDE FOR VENGEANCE

"There are other women in this town," Len said.

"Not like Lola," Will said. "Lenny, you tell him. She's too old for him."

"She's too old for him!" Kyle argued.

"Jesus Christ," Len said, standing up. "I'll tell you what. I'll go and talk to Lola and see which of you she wants. Okay?"

Will and Kyle exchanged glances, then nodded.

"That sounds fair," Kyle said.

"Okay," Will said grudgingly.

"You fellas stay here and play some poker. I'll be back soon."

Len left the cantina. Lola was waiting for him in her room at the hotel.

"Your brothers are funny," Lola said.

"You think so, huh?" Len Lanahan asked.

"They are not at all like you."

"No, they're not."

"Do you take care of them?"

"Yes," Len said. "I promised our mother I would."

"What would they do if they knew you were here with me," she said. "Like this."

"Like this" was both of them naked on her bed, still sweaty from making love.

His brother had been right about one thing. There were no other women like Lola in town. She was tall and full-bodied, with heavy, firm breasts tipped with large brown nipples. She had long legs with heavy thighs—though not *too* heavy—and muscular calves. Around her middle was a slight roll of flesh, due not to age—she was not yet thirty-five—but to the problem of there being nothing else to do in Angelina but eat. If she lost eight, maybe ten pounds, she'd be perfect.

But Len didn't mind her in her present, non-perfect state.

He especially didn't mind it when she was running her hand down over his belly, through his pubic hair until she had wrapped her fingers around his penis.

"They're nice men, really," she said, rubbing her thumb over the swollen head of his penis, "even though Kyle is little more than a boy."

"He won't be for much longer," Len said. "He's coming along." He writhed as he grew in her grasp, and she began to run her hand up and down the length of him.

"And what about Will?"

"Will will never change," Len said. "He'll never grow up."

"You certainly are," she said.

"What?"

"Growing," she said. "So much that in a moment you are going to require all my attention."

For a woman who claimed to have spent her whole life in the town of Angelina she spoke English very well.

"Ah," she said. "See, I told you."

She slid down between his legs and leaned over so she could trap his penis between her big breasts. He'd been sleeping with her for four days now, while his brothers were still arguing over which of them would be the first into her bed.

She rolled him between her breasts, lowering her chin every so often so she could lick the spongy head, and then she moved down a bit so she could take him fully into her mouth.

He had told her that she could sleep with one or both of his brothers if she wanted to, and she said she might do that . . . when she got tired of him.

Only she did not anticipate that happening.
And neither did he.

When Len Lanahan reentered the cantina both Will and Kyle looked up from their poker hand.

"What took so long?" Will asked.

"I had to do a lot of talking," Len said, sitting down with them. "You know, telling her all of your good points—both of you."

"And?"

"She's going to decide soon."

"Tonight?" Will asked.

"No, not tonight."

"Why not?" Kyle asked.

"She's a little too tired tonight," Len said. "Come on, finish that hand and deal me in."

EIGHTEEN

Sam Bigelow couldn't wait to get back to Texas.

Mexico was all right for a short while, but not for any kind of extended stay. Len Lanahan hadn't argued the point with him, because he knew that Bigelow knew enough to keep a low profile once he got back to Texas.

Right now he was in a town called Little Flower, sitting in the cantina over a beer. He was thinking about the Lanahan brothers, wishing that his friend Lenny Lanahan could get out from beneath the other two. The longer he stayed with them, pulling jobs with them, the sooner he was going to get killed. Sam Bigelow felt sure of that.

"*Señor?*"

The voice was right at his elbow. He looked up and saw a woman—a *girl*, really—standing there.

"Yes?"

"You would like some company?"

She was a pretty thing who couldn't have been more than nineteen or twenty. Sam Bigelow was twenty years older than she was.

"Sure," he said, "why not?"

She sat down opposite him. He knew that these local cantina girls were always looking for some rich *gringo* to take them away from it all, and they usually gave their all to impress a man.

She certainly had it to give, he thought. Pert, pointy little breasts and long black hair. Her mouth was full, with a lower lip that looked as if a man could produce nectar by biting into it.

So she was young, so what?

"You want a drink?" he asked.

"Not really, *señor,* but I am required to say yes."

Bigelow looked over at the bartender, who seemed to be watching them.

"Is the bartender your boss?"

She looked over at the hard-eyed bartender, and then said, *"Sí."*

"All right, missy," Bigelow said, "Let's order you a drink then."

When Clint Adams rode into Little Flower, he was once again dragging. As tired and frustrated as he was, however, he refused to give up.

He'd finally found a telegraph line two towns back and had completed an exchange with T.C. that told him that Rick was hanging on. He hadn't improved enough to be operated on, but he hadn't gotten any worse. T.C. had used the word "coma", which Clint was sure had come from the doctor.

Now he left Duke at the livery and headed for the cantina. He'd stop at the hotel afterward. In these sleepy little Mexican towns there was practically no chance that the hotel would be filled up, and the cantina had become his first stop wherever he was.

He entered the cantina and walked to the bar. He ordered a beer and when he got it, turned his back to the bar to look the room over. There were about half a dozen occupied tables in the room, and three or four empties. The tables were taken by Mexicans, all except one. At that one a *gringo* sat with a woman; both of them with drinks before them. The man was sitting with his back to Clint. There was one other girl working the room, a tired-looking Mexican woman who appeared in her late thirties. The seated woman was pretty and young, which was why she was sitting, while the other woman was still on her feet.

The older woman saw him now and headed toward him, obviously intending to try her luck with him.

"Good evening, *señor*," she said, smiling. When she smiled she revealed a gold front tooth which did nothing to enhance her already-waning looks. At one time she might have been an attractive woman, but she'd been working cantinas for too long.

"Good evening," Clint said, wondering how to turn her down without hurting her feelings.

"You are wanting some company?" she asked, pressing her breast against his arm. It was surprisingly firm and he wondered if maybe her body had weathered the years better than her face had.

"Look—" he started to say, but at that point the American sitting with the other girl turned to look at the bar, and Clint saw his face.

"*Señor?*" the woman asked, but he wasn't hearing her.

He was too busy studying the face of Sam Bigelow.

"*Señor?*" the woman said again.

He ignored her, watching as Bigelow—he was *sure* it was Bigelow—and the girl got up and headed for a stairway leading upstairs.

"Where does that go?" Clint asked the woman.

She looked to see what he was talking about and then said with a giggle in her voice, "Upstairs, *señor*. To the rooms."

The "rooms," meaning the rooms where the women

took their customers. He watched as Bigelow and the woman reached the top of the stairs and disappeared.

"Is there another way up there?" he asked her.

"No, *señor*," she said, rubbing her breast against his arm now, "only one." And she giggled again.

He looked at her and made a decision. He put his beer down on the bar, put his arm around her and said, "All right then. Let's go."

"I will make you very happy, *señor*," she said, putting her arm around him and hugging herself to him.

"Just get me up those stairs and I'll be a happy man," he said.

She mistook his words for eagerness to get her in bed and literally dragged him across the room to the stairs.

NINETEEN

When Bigelow entered the room with the girl, he said, "Before you undress, what's your name?"

"Jewel."

Sure, he thought, Jewel. More likely her name was Maria, but these cantina girls rarely used their real names with their customers.

"All right, Jewel," Bigelow said, "now you can undress."

He watched as she took off her blouse and skirt. She had a compact little body. Although her breasts were small, they were firm, with pink nipples that poked out at him impudently. Between her legs was an incredible tangle of wiry black pubic hair and he suddenly found himself with the urge to bury his face in it.

"What would you like to do first, *señor?*" she asked, smiling at him.

Clint allowed himself to be led to a room by the woman, who was gripping his hand tightly.

Once inside, she immediately discarded her clothing, and for a moment he was stunned. The apparent firmness of her breast against his arm had not been at all deceiving. Her body had indeed weathered the passing of time much better than her face had. Her breasts were large and firm, her waist still slim and her legs long and lovely. When she turned for him, he saw that her ass was still firm and well rounded, showing no signs of sag.

"What's your name?" he asked.

"Luisa."

"You have a very beautiful body, Luisa."

"*Gracias, señor.*"

"Under any other circumstances I'd like nothing better than to—"

"Are you interested in that *gringo*?" she asked, a sly look creeping into her eyes.

She was more observant than she had seemed downstairs.

"Yes, I am."

"I can tell you what room he is in."

"Which room is it?"

"I will tell you," she said, then paused before saying, "after."

He studied her body again, and found himself responding to its beauty.

"All right," he said, finally. "After."

After all, Bigelow wasn't going anywhere for a while.

Bigelow liked the way the girl's breasts fit his hands. They were hardly more than a handful for him, but it was like palming two ripe peaches.

She was sitting astride him, his huge erection buried in her to the hilt. As she rode him up and down, breathing hard with the effort, he squeezed her breasts and thumbed her nipples.

The first thing he had done had been to give into his urge. He'd pushed her down on the bed and buried his face between her thighs. With his tongue he'd found her slit and licked and sucked at her until her body was wracked with orgasm, and then he had mounted her. He'd been pounding into her and nearing his own release when she'd said, *"Por favor, señor,* I would like to be on top? Yes?"

He'd turned onto his back then and she had climbed atop him and sat down on his slick penis, swallowing it up again.

Now he pulled her down to him so he could suck her nipples and as he did so she clenched her muscles around him, yanking his seed from him in long, almost painful bursts.

Luisa was an incredibly eager sex partner.

Clint felt sorry for any man who had judged her by her appearance and passed up an invitation to her room.

For the time he spent with her he literally forgot about Sam Bigelow being in another room nearby.

First he had kissed and sucked her breasts and nipples, bringing her to a small orgasm that way, and then had used his mouth to explore her body.

"Aiee, señor," she said at one point, "you make me feel as no man has ever done before."

It could have been something she said to all of her customers, but at that moment he didn't particularly care.

After he had familiarized himself with every orifice of her body, he mounted her and drove himself into her. She caught her breath and wrapped her powerful legs around his waist. She held on for dear life as he pounded into her and as he began to spurt inside her, she bit her lips and achieved her own orgasm . . .

• • •

Jewel knelt in front of Sam Bigelow and sucked his penis avidly. She had started to do it while they were lying down, but he had told her that he wanted her to do it on her knees in front of him while he was standing.

"Whatever you wish, *señor*," she told him. "A man with a tool as beautiful as this—" and she tightened her hold on him—"can have whatever he wants from a woman."

"Yeah, yeah," he said, dismissing her words as whore-talk, "just get to it."

And get to it she did. She suckled his penis like it was a salt lick and she was an animal. He grunted as she cupped his balls in her hand, took him deep into her throat and once again pulled his orgasm from him . . .

Luisa was on her hands and knees on the bed, with her shapely butt hiked up into the air. Clint knelt behind her and she spread her legs slightly. He slid though the smooth warm flesh of her thighs and up inside her.

"*Dios mio!*" she cried. She reached out and grasped the bedpost with both hands as he began to pulse into her.

This had been by her request and although he had met many women who enjoyed intercourse in this manner, Luisa seemed to especially relish it, and he certainly didn't mind giving it to her.

Lying on his back with "Jewel" in the crook of his arm, Sam Bigelow was once again thinking about Len Lanahan. Maybe he should have stayed with Lenny, but they had always gone their own way after a job. Maybe that was one reason they worked so well together. Maybe that was why Lenny preferred his company to that of his own brothers.

After all, he was around Will and Kyle all the time. If Bigelow and Lenny Lanahan were around each other all the time, maybe they wouldn't get along so well anymore.

"*Señor?*"

"Yeah?"

She rubbed her hand over his massive chest and said, "I have never been with a man so large as you. I thought you would hurt me."

"I wouldn't do that," he said. "I don't hurt women."

"No, I do not mean on purpose. I mean . . . because you are so big . . . here . . ." She slid her hand beneath the sheet and took hold of his flaccid penis. "Even as soft as this you are larger than most men."

"I wouldn't know that," he said. "I don't make a habit of looking at other men there."

"Then you must take my word for it, *señor*," she said, stroking him so that he began to harden again.

"Again?" she asked.

"Yes," he said, as he continued to grow in her hand, "again."

"Now will you tell me what room the other *gringo* is in?" Clint asked.

"*Sí, señor,*" Luisa said dreamily. She was lying next to him, her leg and thigh resting on one of his, her hand on his penis. He slid his own hand down so that he was cupping one of her smooth buttocks.

"I know that I am not beautiful, like Jewel," she said to Clint, "or so young, but you have made me very happy this night, *Señor Clint*."

"You gave me a lot of pleasure, too, Luisa," he assured her.

"I am happy that you came here with me," she said. "Jewel gets all the . . . the desirable men. I get the . . . the pigs, the ones who have no desire to make *me* feel pleasure, only to take their own."

"They're foolish men," he said. "You have as much to offer as Jewel—perhaps more."

"More?"

"Experience."

"Ah . . ."

"Now, Luisa," Clint said, "which room are Jewel and the other *gringo* in?"

TWENTY

Luisa opened the door to the room and looked out into the hall.

"Come," she said to Clint. "The way is clear."

He came up behind her and they entered the hallway together.

He had told her to just tell him what room the man was in, but she insisted on taking him to the room herself.

"There are no numbers on the doors," she said. "You might make a mistake."

In the end he agreed.

She led him down the hall, nearer to the staircase than her room was.

"There," she whispered, pointing, "that one."

"All right," he said. "Go downstairs."

She shook her head.

"I will wait in my room. If something goes wrong, you can come there."

"All right," he said. He agreed because he just wanted to get her out of the hall.

She smiled, giving him a flash of gold before scampering down the hall the way they had come.

It was unfortunate, that gold tooth.

Inside the room in question Sam Bigelow was getting dressed.

"You will not stay the night?" Jewel asked.

"No."

"Will you . . . come back?"

"No," Bigelow said. "I'll be leaving in the morning, Jewel."

"You would not . . . take me with you, would you?" she asked.

He looked at her for a moment, lying in bed, still naked.

Hell, he thought, why not? For a while, anyway.

"Sure, Jewel," he said. "Pack your things and be ready to leave in the morning."

"Truly?" she asked. "You mean it?"

"Of course I mean it."

She smiled happily, clapping her hands together in glee.

"Oh, Sam—"

"Just be ready," he said, and walked to the door.

As Clint approached the door he saw the doorknob begin to turn. Quickly he looked around for someplace to hide. He moved to a door on the other side and turned the knob. It opened and he slipped inside, leaving the door open a crack.

He watched as Sam Bigelow left the room across the way, closing the door behind him. He debated whether or not he should confront Bigelow in the hall, and then decided against it. In the event of trouble, there was no way of knowing how the men in the cantina would react, who they would side with.

He allowed Bigelow to go to the steps and start down, and then left the room and moved to the head of the stairs. He waited until he saw Bigelow go through the front doors, then hurried down the stairs.

The only place Bigelow could possibly be going was the hotel.

TWENTY-ONE

Clint left the cantina and saw Sam Bigelow walking toward the hotel. It was dark out, and he kept to the shadows as he followed the big man.

When Bigelow entered the hotel, Clint waited long enough for the man to reach his room, and then walked into the hotel.

As Clint entered, the desk clerk looked up at him. From the look on the man's face he knew trouble was brewing. He slid out from behind the desk and tried to slip past Clint, who caught his arm.

"*Señor, por favor,*" the man said, frightened.

"Just tell me what room the other *gringo* is in," Clint said, "and you can go."

"*Seis,*" the frightened man said. "Six."

"Go," Clint said, releasing the man's arm.

The man ran out into the street. He was either going for help, or he was just going for cover.

Clint mounted the steps and climbed to the second floor. He hadn't taken a room himself, yet, so he didn't know the layout of the hotel, but as it turned out it was no different from any other hotel: a long hallway lined with doors. All he had to do was find the one with a "6" on it—only there were no numbers on the doors!

Annoyed because he had let the desk clerk go he started moving down the hall, listening at the doors. He didn't know what he was listening for. Did *gringos* make different sounds than Mexicans behind closed doors?

Behind one door he heard the unmistakable sounds of someone having sex very energetically. Considering where Bigelow had just come from, he decided that he could rule that room out.

Moving along to the next three rooms he heard nothing. He decided to consider the four doors he'd already pressed his ears to as rooms 1, 2, 3, and 4. He pressed his ear to the door of room 5, and heard nothing but deep breathing. He decided that Bigelow could not have fallen asleep that quickly.

As it turned out, the hallway only had six doors. Behind the sixth he heard the sound of movement. He listened a little longer, and when he heard the sound of bedsprings he pressed his back against the opposite wall and kicked out at the door.

The door slammed open and he lunged into the room. Immediately a viselike arm slid around his neck and held his head fast.

"Drop the gun or I'll break your neck," a man's voice said into his ear.

Clint dropped his gun.

"Kick it under the bed."

Reluctantly Clint did as he was told, cursing himself for a fool. He'd underestimated Bigelow; the man had been waiting for him.

Suddenly, the arm moved away from his neck and he could move his head, and breathe easier. He was about to speak when he was hit from behind. The blow was to his back, and it propelled him forward, where he sprawled onto the bed.

He turned and stared up at the big man, whose hands were empty. His gun was still in its holster.

Now maybe *he* was underestimating Clint, not knowing who he was.

"Suppose you tell me, friend, why I shouldn't kill you," Bigelow said.

"How about I'd be very upset about it?" Clint asked.

"You're a funny man," Bigelow said, "but that wouldn't be good enough."

"I didn't think it would."

"What's your name?"

If Clint told this man his real name while he had the drop on him like this, he'd be a dead man.

He gave the man the first name that came to his mind.

"Hickok."

Bigelow gave him a pitying look and said, "Your sense of humor is going to get you killed."

"Listen," Clint said, helplessly, "that's my name, Ben Hickok. No relation, really."

"No," Bigelow said, studying Clint critically, "I wouldn't think so. Well, why were you following me? Robbery?"

Clint smiled what he hoped was a sheepish smile.

"I am a little down on my luck."

"And you planned to rob a fellow American?"

"Did you ever know a Mexican worth robbing?"

Bigelow laughed at this.

"You got a point, pilgrim, you know that?"

"I was hoping . . ."

"Well, I guess I could kill you," Bigelow said, "or cripple you up a little—"

"If I have a vote—"

"You don't!" Bigelow said, his eyes turning cold. "I can sympathize with a fella down on his luck, friend, but my sympathy ends with a guy who was gonna rob me, and probably kill me, as well!"

"Hey," Clint said, trying to sound hurt, "I may be a lot of things, but I ain't a killer—especially not a fellow American."

"Sorry, friend," Sam Bigelow said, "but that won't wash. Now I got to make my choice."

"Well, then, you better kill me."

"Why?" Bigelow asked, looking surprised. "Why not bust you up a little?"

"Because," Clint said, sitting up on the bed so that his feet were on the floor, "if you get close enough to me, you'll be the one who gets busted up. No, you'd better kill me from where you stand, friend. That's what I'd do if I was you."

Clint knew he was taking a big chance—two big chances. The first was that Bigelow might take him at his word and shoot him from where he stood.

The second chance was that Bigelow would take the challenge, because Clint didn't know if he could take the big man.

He saw the sparkle in Bigelow's eyes and knew he had him.

"That sounds like a challenge."

"Take it any way you like," Clint said. He decided to stay silent after that and not press the point.

"Get up, friend," Bigelow said. "I think I'm gonna have to teach you a lesson."

"You gonna shoot me?" Clint said, standing. He kept his hand on the pillow.

"I'm gonna beat some sense into you," Bigelow said. As he took a step forward, Clint picked up the pillow and threw in into the man's face.

Bigelow raised his hands to ward off the pillow and Clint moved forward very quickly. He lifted his leg, bent his knee, and sent the heel of his boot crashing into Bigelow's belly.

Lucky for Clint, Bigelow was in his forties, and his belly wasn't as hard as it had once been. The air whooshed out of the man's lungs as he was bent double by the blow. Gagging, he started to reach for his gun.

Clint's gun was out of sight and out of reach beneath the bed, so he quickly moved again, kicking Bigelow in the head. The man's eyes rolled up into his head, and he fell over.

It struck Clint that he'd been very lucky lately in scrapes with men bigger than he was.

If anyone asked him how his luck was going recently, his answer would undoubtedly be, "Can't kick!"

TWENTY-TWO

"I'm impressed," Clint said.

Sam Bigelow sat up and put his hand to his head.

"You like to killed me," he said.

"Not hardly," Clint said. "You've got a hard head."

Bigelow was still on the floor, Clint had decided that he was too heavy to try and move. Instead he'd simply retrieved his gun from beneath the bed and left Bigelow's in its place, then he searched the man for other weapons, finding none. After that he took the man's saddlebags—which were filled with his share of the money from the bank robbery—and just sat back on a straight-backed chair and waited for the man to wake up.

Now that he was awake, Bigelow made as if to rise and Clint said, "Uh-uh, don't do that."

Bigelow looked at Clint and said, "Come on, man, we're even. You go your way and I'll go mine."

"No."

"What do you mean, no?"

"You haven't given me what I want, yet."

Bigelow frowned and sat back down on the floor.

"If you wanted to rob me you could have done it while I was unconscious."

"That's true."

"What do you want, then?" Bigelow asked. "Who the hell are you?"

"My name is Adams, Clint Adams."

"Adams—" Bigelow said, "You mean . . . the Gunsmith?"

Clint simply shrugged.

"Well," Bigelow said, "I guess the joke's on me, huh? You sure fooled me."

"Sorry."

"So, what do you want if you don't want to rob me?"

"Oh, I'm going to take your money, all right," Clint said, patting the man's saddlebags.

"You *are* gonna rob me?" the man asked, incredulous. "I heard a lot of things about you, but not that you were a thief."

"Considering where this money came from, I'd consider that the pot calling the kettle black."

"Wha— Oh . . . oh!" Bigelow said, as what he thought must be the truth dawned on him. "You taken to bounty hunting now, is that it?"

"Nope," Clint said, shaking his head.

"What then?" Bigelow said, thoroughly confused.

"You and your friends left a friend of mine behind pretty badly wounded."

"Friend?" Bigelow asked. "The sheriff and his deputy?"

"No."

"Oh, the jasper with the shotgun."

"That's the one."

"Jesus, man, he come out of nowhere. We fired in self-defense."

"While robbing a bank."

"Shit, that's our business."

"And everybody's got to do something for a living, right?"

"Right . . ."

"Wrong," Clint said. "I want your friends, Bigelow. I want the Lanahan brothers."

"Well, I don't know where they are. I split from them a ways back."

"Well, you know *where* you split from them," Clint said. "Tell me that."

When the man didn't reply immediately, Clint figured he was fixing to lie.

He took his gun out of his holster and cocked the hammer back. The sound echoed in the small room, and Bigelow jumped.

"What the—"

"If you lie to me I'm going to shoot you in the kneecap. If you lie again, I'll shoot you in the other kneecap. If you still lie, we'll start with your elbows. You ever see a man flopping around on the floor with no control of his arms and legs? It isn't a pretty sight."

"Hey, hey . . . wait," Bigelow said, breathlessly, "let me think—"

"If you think, you're going to lie," Clint said. "Answer the question. Where did you and the Lanahans part company?"

"Bonita," Bigelow said, "a town called Bonita."

"That's more like it."

Bigelow frowned and said, "How do you know I ain't lying?"

Clint frowned and said, "You wouldn't lie to a fellow American, would you, Sam?"

Clint marched Sam Bigelow over to the local sheriff,

where he was greeted without courtesy.

"I am sorry, *señor*," the sheriff said, "but I cannot extend to you the hospitality of my jail."

"Why not?"

"This man has committed no crime in my country."

"But I'm telling you he robbed a bank and killed two men in the United States."

"What he did in *Los Estados Unidos* is not my concern, *señor*."

"What about some common courtesy—"

"*Señor*," the man said, patiently, "you admit that you are not a lawman of your country. What kind of common courtesy are you referring to? No, *señor*. Please, take your private argument and leave my town, *por favor*."

"Look—" Clint began, but the sheriff turned a deaf ear to him.

Clint gave Sam Bigelow a sour look, made even more sour by the fact that the big man was smiling broadly.

"Come on," he said, pushing the big man toward the door.

Out on the street, Bigelow, still smiling, said, "All right, give me my gun and my money and we'll say good-bye here."

"Jesus, Sam, even if I gave you your gun I wouldn't give you the money. It's not yours."

"It is, too," Bigelow said indignantly, "I stole it!"

"Forget it," Clint said, "I'm not giving you your gun or the money."

"Then what are you going to do?" Bigelow demanded. "Take me with you?"

"That's exactly what I'm going to do," Clint said, "take you with me."

"You can't do that," Bigelow said.

"Sam, either I take you with me, or I bury you."

Without hesitation Sam Bigelow said, "When do we leave?"

As they rode out of town, Bigelow with his hands tied at the wrists, but tied in front of him so that he could maneuver his horse, Bigelow said, "How come you're looking for the Lanahan brothers and not the other man?"

The question about the other man verified what Clint had thought about the sixth man. Either Rick or one of the dead lawmen must have wounded the sixth man, who had subsequently died, leaving five men to split the take.

"I found the other man already," Clint replied.

"And what did he tell you?" Bigelow said.

"Nothing," Clint said, giving Bigelow a pointed look, "he couldn't tell me anything, at all."

TWENTY-THREE

Clint Adams and Sam Bigelow rode into Bonita three days later. By now Clint had combined the money he'd taken from Yates with the money he'd taken from Sam Bigelow, and had over eleven thousand dollars for his trouble . . .

"Why don't you just keep all that money and let me go?" Bigelow had suggested when they camped the first night.

"Forget it," Clint said, counting the money.

"You got a real bad honest streak, huh?"

Clint stared at Bigelow.

"I've got a friend lying near death with a bullet in his chest, and wounds from being trampled by horses. You and *your* friends rode right over him after you shot him." Clint shook his head then and said, "What am I talking about? You probably don't know what a friend is."

"Hey," Bigelow said, "I may be a thief, but I got feelings. I know about friendship."

"Yeah," Clint said, finishing his count, "I can see that. I notice a small imbalance between your share and your friend Yates'."

"I didn't do the divvying," Bigelow said. "That was Lenny."

"Lanahan?"

"Yeah."

"He's the older brother, right?" Clint said. "The leader?"

"That's right. If he thought I should get some extra, that was his business. I didn't ask what anybody got."

"It's been my experience that these jobs are usually split evenly."

"What do you know about bank robbers?" Bigelow asked.

"I've arrested enough of you bastards in my time," Clint said.

"Oh, that's right. You were a lawman for a while, weren't you?"

"A long time ago."

"What happened?"

Clint was stuffing the money into one saddlebag as he looked at Bigelow.

"I got tired of it."

"I guess you would get tired of putting men behind bars," Bigelow said, as if he understood that a man could only take so much of that.

"That wasn't it," Clint said. "I never got tired of putting you bastards behind bars, it was the treatment I used to get from the law-abiding citizens that I got tired of."

Bigelow pointed a finger at Clint and said, "That's the second time you called me a bastard. I had a maw and a paw, Adams, and if you call me that again I'm coming across this fire at you."

The two men locked eyes for a few moments, and then the Gunsmith did something that surprised Sam Bigelow.

He apologized.

"Sorry, Sam."

Taken aback Bigelow said, "Yeah, well, that's all right. Tell me how the law-abiding citizens treated you?"

"Ah," Clint said in disgust, "you've never been a lawman, Sam. You never had to try and get up a posse from a bunch of no-account townspeople. They figure they hired you to do that job, and it wasn't none of their concern to try and help you."

Sam Bigelow nodded and said, "Yeah, I guess a man could get tired of that—but tell me, what kept you from going bad after that?"

"I may have been tired of upholding the law, Sam, but I sure wasn't ready to start breaking it."

"Maybe I never been a lawman, Clint," Bigelow said, "but I'll bet you ain't never been rich."

"No, I can't say that I have."

"I have, a lot of times."

"And then?"

"I spend it. Jesus, that's what money's for."

"If you'd saved some of it you'd be so rich now you wouldn't have to pull any more jobs."

"Hell, that's what I do, Clint," Sam Bigelow said. "I couldn't be no man of leisure. Naw, I go through money as fast as I get it, and I enjoy every minute of it—then I go out and get some more."

"You mean you steal some more," Clint said. "Can't you see that you're nothing more than a common thief, Sam?"

"Well," Bigelow said then, "if you're gonna get insulting again, I'm finished talking . . ."

Now they rode into Bonita down the main street until they came to livery. During that ride, though, Clint had seen enough to realize what kind of town Bonita was.

When they got to the livery they both dismounted.

"Give me your hands, Sam," Clint said.

Sam extended his hands and Clint took off the rope that had been on the big man's wrists for three days.

"What—" Bigelow started to say, but he stopped when Clint took out the man's gun and handed it to him.

"Put that in your holster."

"What the hell—" Bigelow said, holstering his gun. "You're letting me go?"

"Not hardly," Clint said. "You must think I'm a real fool, Sam."

"I don't know—"

"I know a rogue town when I see one, Sam," Clint said. "This town is full of thieves and cutthroats and has no law. Did you really think I'd let you walk around with your hands tied, making everyone think I was a lawman? I'd have been dead in five seconds."

"I guess I should have known better, huh?"

"I guess you should have. Now, if you're thinking of trying anything with that gun, don't . . . it's empty."

Bigelow looked down at the gun in his holster.

"What the hell good is an empty gun?"

"None."

"And if there's trouble?"

"I'll handle it—that is, unless you start it."

"Why would I—"

"Maybe you still have an idea that you can get me killed here," Clint said, "Don't, because at the first sign of trouble—trouble that *you* started—I'll put a bullet in your head. You understand?"

"I understand," Bigelow said tightly. "Just as long as you know that the first chance I get I'll be all over you."

"Why, Sam," Clint said, "if you felt any other way I'd be downright disappointed in you."

"Yeah . . ."

"All right," Clint said, "let's get these horses bedded down and then get something to eat."

TWENTY-FOUR

"You've been here before," Clint said. "Where's a good place to eat?"

"You find out."

"Hey," Clint said, "it's your stomach, too."

"Well," Bigelow said, "I've never been afraid to admit when you had a point. There's a small cafe down the street here."

"Should we get a hotel room first?"

"Hotel rooms are first come first served," Bigelow said. "If you don't get one you just have to find someplace around town."

"I see," Clint said. "We might as well eat, then."

"Why not?"

Bigelow led the way to the cafe, which was about half full since it was really after lunchtime.

"Take a table anywhere," a harried-looking man in his fifties told them.

"That's Bates," Bigelow said as they took a table.

"How many times have you been here?"

"Once," Bigelow answered before thinking. "Afraid I might have some friends here?"

"The thought had entered my mind," Clint said, but he felt that Bigelow's reply had been a truthful one. If he'd been here only once, the chances were good they wouldn't run into any friends of his.

"What should we order?" Clint asked.

"The stew."

"Is that a specialty?"

"It's what I had last time, and it was decent."

"How's the coffee?"

"Strong."

"Good. Let's get a pot."

"Whatever you say," Bigelow said. "You're paying."

"I am?"

"You took all of my money."

"So I did."

"Here comes Jess."

"Jess?" Clint said. He turned his head and saw an attractive woman in her thirties approaching the table. She was tall and lithe, with shoulder-length brown hair. As she approached them Clint saw that she was more than just attractive.

"She's Bates' wife."

"*She's* married to—"

"Yes," Bigelow said, and then she was at their table.

"Bigelow," she said, obviously recognizing him. "Couldn't stay away, huh?"

"Not from you, darlin'."

"Who's your friend?"

Before Bigelow could answer Clint said, "My name is Clint."

"Glad to meet you, Clint. What will you boys have?"

"We'll have some of your good stew, Jess," Bigelow said.

"The stew is Bates'," she said. She looked at Clint

and said, "He's the cook, I'm just the waitress."

"Yeah, but nobody gives service like you do, Jess," Bigelow said.

A look passed between them and Clint thought that maybe Bigelow'd gotten more than just table service from Jess Bates the last time he was here.

"I'll get your stew," she said.

"And a pot of coffee."

"Oh, the coffee," she said. "That's mine. I hope you like it strong."

"I love it strong," Clint said.

"Good. I'll be right back."

As she walked away, both men watched her hips sway. From the front all you saw was her apron, but from the back they could see how tightly her jeans fit.

"How did she come to be married to Bates?" Clint wondered aloud.

"I don't know," Bigelow said. "We, uh, didn't do much talking the last time I was here."

"I'll bet," Clint said. "Well, I'll say one thing for you, Sam."

"What?"

"You've got good taste in women."

"Thanks."

"Can't say much for her taste in men, though . . ."

"Thanks . . ."

While she was collecting their plates after their meal Jess asked, "How long are you . . . and your friend . . . going to be here this time, Sam?"

"Probably just overnight," Clint replied, before Bigelow could.

"Oh," she said, sounding somewhat disappointed.

She looked at Clint and said, "That won't give us much time to get acquainted, will it?"

It took him a moment before he realized that she was speaking to him.

"Uh, no, no I guess not."

"Pity," she said, and walked away, her hips twitching like two dogs in a sack.

As they left the cafe Bigelow said, "Looks like I'm yesterday's news."

"Too bad we're not going to be here a little longer."

"You were right about one thing, though."

"What's that?"

"Her lousy taste in men."

TWENTY-FIVE

They went to the hotel and found that they had a few rooms available.

"Things must be slow," Clint remarked.

The clerk responded with a scowl.

"Sign in?" Clint asked.

"Why?" the clerk said. He handed Clint a key and said, "A room for your friend?"

"No, we'll share."

"There's only one bed."

"He'll sleep on the floor."

"Like a dog," Bigelow added.

"Heel," Clint said, and propelled Bigelow toward the stairway.

"What's that mean?" Bigelow asked as they ascended.

"What?"

"Heel?"

"It means heel," Clint said. "It's what you say to a dog."

Bigelow frowned in puzzlement and said, "I thought you kicked dogs."

"*You* kick dogs," Clint said. "I kick—"

"Never mind," Bigelow said. "I have a feeling you're going to get insulting again."

They got to their room, and Clint looked at the bed.

"See why I didn't object to sleeping on the floor?"

The bed was little more than a pallet.

"You might have to fight me for it," Clint said, dumping the saddlebags on it.

Bigelow went over to the lone chair in the room and sat in it. It creaked, but held.

"I'm gonna give it one more try, Clint."

Clint stared at Sam Bigelow, wondering when they had gotten on a first-name basis. Hell, he may have even been the one who started it. Against his better judgment he knew he liked the guy.

"What?" Clint asked. "Try what?"

"The money," Bigelow said, pointing to the saddlebags. "We split the money, and go our separate ways."

"Aw," Clint said, "just when I was beginning to like you."

"You know, that's the problem," Bigelow said, leaning forward. "I'm starting to like you, too. Maybe we could be partners."

"Doing what?"

Bigelow shrugged.

"Whatever pays."

"I don't work that way."

"You mean you never have worked that way," Bigelow said. "There's always a first time."

"Not for me."

"All right," Bigelow said, "what happens when we catch up to the Lanahans? There are three of them. Counting me, that's four."

"That's very good," Clint said. "You had some schooling, I see."

Bigelow went on, undaunted.

"How are you gonna get all four of us back to Texas?" he asked.

Clint shrugged and said, "Slung over your horses?"

"Uh-uh," Bigelow said. "You don't work that way."

"You mean I never *have* worked that way," Clint said. "There's always a first time."

Bigelow studied Clint and then said, "Yeah, I guess there is always a first time."

"Are you ready to go get a drink?"

"Sure," Bigelow said, standing up, "why not?"

As they headed for the door, Bigelow stopped and said, "Hey, wait, are you gonna leave the money here?"

"Why not?"

"Somebody'll steal it, that's why!"

"In a town full of thieves?" Clint asked. "You mean there's no honor—"

"Hey, stop foolin' around," Bigelow said. "Somebody's gonna steal that money!"

"And what happens if we start walking around town carrying those saddlebags around? You don't think someone's not going to start thinking that maybe there's something in there that's worth something?"

Bigelow thought a moment and said, "You got a point there, Clint . . . but how about we tuck it down under the bed, just in case."

"You just want me to bend over so you can try to kick me in the head," Clint said.

"What kind of thing is that to say?" Bigelow asked, looking hurt.

"Never mind," Clint said. "You want it under the bed, you put it there."

Bigelow grabbed the saddlebags and bent over to stick them under the bed, muttering, "Never saw anybody so untrusting before in my life . . ."

"You ready to go?" Clint asked.

Bigelow stood up, wiped his palms clean on his pants and said, "Yeah, I'm ready to go."

Across the street two men stood in a doorway and watched Clint Adams and Sam Bigelow leave the hotel.

"Are you sure it's him?" Walter Creedence asked Al Dubbing.

"Sure I'm sure," Dubbing said. "I know the goddamn Gunsmith when I see him."

"And who's the other fella?"

"Him I don't know," Dubbing said.

"All right," Creedence said. "It don't matter, anyway. Should we do this alone?"

"Stupid!" Dubbing said. "I just told you that's the goddamn Gunsmith! Go and find Stillman and Milsap and I'll keep an eye on him. I don't want him to get away."

"Why are we doing this?" Creedence wanted to know. "It ain't as if there's a price on his head or nothing."

"Listen, he put my brother in the ground two years ago," Dubbing said. "That's reason enough, but just think of the rep the men who put the Gunsmith in the ground are gonna have, huh?"

"Okay," Creedence said. "I'll find Stillman and Milsap, and then we'll find you."

"And then we'll get it done," Al Dubbing said, "and we'll get it done right."

TWENTY-SIX

Clint and Bigelow each got a beer and took a table toward the back of the cantina.

"This is a big place for a nothing town," Clint said. The cantina had about twenty tables, and three girls working the place.

"They do a lot of business."

"I guess so . . ." Clint said, although at the moment the place was only about half full.

"When it gets dark this place will be full up," Bigelow said.

"And we'll leave," Clint said. "We'll be better off staying in our room until morning, and we'll get an early start."

"Look at these two ladies coming over to us," Bigelow said. "What do you say we take them back to the room with us?"

"We only have one bed, Sam, remember?" Clint reminded him. "That is, if you can call it that."

"We can use the floor," Bigelow said. "Hell, if you pay these girls enough they'll do it on the hotel roof, hanging from their heels."

"I don't pay for it, Sam."

"What?"

Clint looked at him and shook his head.

"Never."

"Why not?"

"There's enough of it walking around free."

"You boys looking for some company?" one of the girls asked.

She was an American, while the other girl was a Mexican. Clint was surprised. First Jess, who was American, and now another one. He would have thought all the women in this town would be Mexican.

The American had dirty blonde hair and smooth white shoulders, while the Mexican girl had black hair and dark skin. They made quite a contrast, especially since the blonde was near five foot ten, while the Mexican was barely five feet tall.

Under other circumstances Clint might have liked to take them both to his room—alone.

"Company?" the Mexican girl repeated.

"No," Clint said.

"Yes," Bigelow said.

The blonde frowned and said, "Well, which is it, boys?"

"My friend here doesn't like to pay for his company," Bigelow explained.

"Well," the blonde said, "considering how slow it is in here, we might be able to make an exception—for him."

"You like to pay?" the Mexican asked Bigelow.

"Well, honey," Bigelow said, "I wouldn't say I like to pay, but I can't say I mind, either. Kind of adds some spice to the, uh, relationship, don't you think?"

"I think," the Mexican girl said.

"Unfortunately," Bigelow went on, "my friend here

controls all of the cash, right now."

"And he doesn't pay," the blonde said.

"Right," Bigelow said.

"Maybe you're just unsociable?" the blonde asked Clint.

Right at that moment the batwing doors of the cantina opened and four men came walking in. One of them looked around, spotted Clint and Bigelow, and said something to the other three.

"Honey, what's your name?" Clint asked.

"Mona," the blonde said. "This here's Rosa."

"Well, Mona, I think you've got just about the prettiest white skin I've seen in a long time . . ."

"Why, thank you—"

". . . and if our situation was a little different, I'd show you how unsociable I really am."

"What's wrong with your situation?" she asked.

"Yeah," Bigelow said, "what's wrong with our situation?"

Clint inclined his head toward the four men who had just entered and said, "It's just taken a turn for the worse."

Bigelow looked at the four men who had entered and said, "They don't look any meaner than most."

"Except for one thing," Clint said.

"What?"

"I know one of them."

"Who?"

"Fella named Al Dubbing."

"How do you know him?"

"I killed his brother two years ago."

"And he remembers you?"

"Oh, he remembers, all right."

"You ladies better stand aside," Bigelow said.

Rosa shook her head sadly and said, "Too many *gringos*."

"Well, Rosa, honey," Clint said, "there's likely to be a few less in a few moments."

The women started to move aside and Bigelow stood up and said, "Wait for me, ladies."

"Where are you going?" Clint asked.

"My gun's empty, remember?" Bigelow asked Clint. "And you said you'd handle any trouble that came along—and this trouble is of your doing, not mine." Bigelow picked up his glass and said, "I'll take my beer over here with the ladies and watch with interest."

"Sure," Clint said, "and hope they kill me."

"Well," Bigelow said, "it would leave the money for me, wouldn't it?"

"Yeah, it would," Bigelow said, "but I gotta tell you, Clint, I'm kind of hoping you'll live up to your reputation. I've never seen one man take four, before. It'll be a sight to behold."

Yep, Clint thought, it sure would be.

Sam Bigelow couldn't lose, either way.

He wished he could say the same thing about himself.

TWENTY-SEVEN

Dubbing saw Clint Adams and turned to talk to his companions.

"That's him," he said.

"The great Gunsmith," Dan Milsap said. "He don't look like much."

"I've seen him take two men at once," Dubbing said.

"I heard of a time he took three," Frankie Stillman said.

"Maybe we should have brought more men," Creedence commented.

"Nonsense," Milsap said. "Four of us is plenty."

"Let's get it done, then," Creedence said.

"I've been waiting two years for this," Al Dubbing said. "I'll talk to him first. I want him to know who's killing him."

As Bigelow and the two women moved to the bar, Clint pushed his chair back from the table. He watched as Al Dubbing approached.

"You remember me, Adams?" Dubbing asked.

"I remember you, Dubbing."

"You remember my brother?"

"I remember he was a fool," Clint said. "Do you plan on being one, too?"

"He was a fool because he tried to take you on his own," Dubbing said. "I'm not alone, Adams."

"No, I can see that."

"I want you to know who's going to kill you."

"Dubbing," Clint said, "no matter what happens, I'll kill you first. You won't live to see me die."

Dubbing licked his lips, which had suddenly grown very dry.

"As long as you're dead," he said.

"But how will you know?" Clint asked.

"I—I'll know."

"Then get back there with your friends, Dubbing. Let's get this over with."

Dubbing licked his lips again, then backed away from the table until he was standing with the other three men. It bothered him that Clint Adams did not look nervous, or worried.

He was too damned calm!

"Aren't you going to help him?" Mona whispered to Bigelow.

"He doesn't need any help," Bigelow said to her. "Think you can get me another beer, honey?"

"Sure . . ."

Clint stood up and stepped away from the table. The four men facing him spread out, arm's length from one another.

Everyone else in the cantina stood up and pushed to one side or the other, out of the line of fire.

Clint watched Dubbing, figuring that the others would

key on him. When he moved, Clint would kill him, and then take his chances with the other men.

Bigelow watched Al Dubbing, the man who had spoken to Clint Adams. He wondered if the Gunsmith could actually outdraw and kill four men. Had anyone ever done it? Had Hickok?

It was a tall order, even for the Gunsmith.

As Al Dubbing went for his gun, Sam Bigelow threw his beer mug at the man nearest him.

As Dubbing went for his gun, Clint became dimly aware of a beer mug flying through the air. He had no time to follow it, however. He drew and fired at Dubbing first.

Dubbing felt the bullet enter his chest and all the strength left his body. He felt himself falling and he tried to live . . . even if it was just long enough to see Adams die . . .

Live, he screamed at himself . . .

Live, damn it . . .

Clint moved to his left after he fired the first shot, and then fired again at the man on Dubbing's left. As that man fell, he moved and fired again, and the third man staggered.

He swiveled to look at the fourth man and found him on his knees, his forehead bleeding. There was a beer mug on the floor near him, empty now, and he was covered with beer.

He looked up, saw Clint looking at him, and began to reach for his gun.

"Don't!" Clint shouted.

The man stopped short, then continued, grabbing his gun in panic.

The Gunsmith shot him.

Clint looked over at Bigelow, sure that it was he who had thrown the beer mug.

Bigelow spread his big hands and said, "Oops, clumsy me."

TWENTY-EIGHT

After the bodies had been hauled away, Clint joined Bigelow at the bar. The big man, still flanked by both Mona and Rosa, handed Clint a mug of beer.

"Thanks."

"Thank Mona," Bigelow said. "The beer is on her."

"No," Clint said, "I meant for the other beer."

"Oh, that," Bigelow said. "Couldn't help it. It slipped out of my hand."

"All the way over to there?"

Bigelow shrugged and said, "The mug was slippery."

Clint felt the mug in his hand, and it was wet and slippery.

"Sure," he said, sipping his beer.

"Ladies, could we have a few moments," Bigelow said to the girls.

"Sure," Mona said. "Come on, Rosa." She gave both men a pointed look and said, "We'll be back." She looked particularly excited by the events that had taken place.

"Gunplay has that effect on some women," Bigelow said. "Still not interested?"

"It wouldn't work," Clint said. "Not all four of us in the same room."

"There *are* other rooms available at the hotel."

"Let you go into another room alone?" Clint said. "How long would you stay?"

"After what I did here you still don't trust me?" Bigelow asked. "I'm deeply wounded."

"Sam—"

"Look, Clint," Sam Bigelow said, "I'm not about to run out on all that money, not after I worked so hard to get it. I want to go along with you and find the Lanahan brothers. I want this to be resolved."

Clint studied Sam Bigelow. The man had as good as saved his life, even though he thought that he could have shot the fourth man, as well. None of the four of them had been particularly fast.

"I'll need your gun," he said.

"I have no bullets."

"You could get bullets."

Bigelow smiled and said, "In this town, I could very easily get another gun—but if I wanted you dead, I could have let them do it."

"You have a point."

"It's about time," Bigelow said. "You've been having all of them up to now."

Clint looked over at the two women, who were watching them intently. The blonde was licking her lips and absently stroking the flesh of her arm with the fingers of her left hand.

"Which one do you want?" Clint asked.

Sam Bigelow smiled and said, "Take your pick."

TWENTY-NINE

Clint, Bigelow, Mona, and Rosa all walked to the hotel together. When they entered the desk clerk looked up and gave them a bored stare.

"Is there an extra room?" Clint asked.

"There are a lot of extra rooms."

"Can we have one?"

"Take your pick," the man said, and then looked back down at the book he was reading.

They went upstairs to the second floor and entered their room. Rosa had attached herself to Bigelow, while Mona was on Clint's arm.

As they entered, Jess Bates looked up at them from the bed. She was sitting with her back against the bedpost with one leg bent at the knee. She was wearing an old man's shirt, and her tight jeans, and she looked infinitely better in them than did the two cantina girls in their dresses.

"Well," Jess said, smiling at them, "this has all the makings of a fun evening."

Mona and Rosa glared at Jess, who simply smiled back at them.

"How are we going to do this?" she asked. "This bed can barely fit two, let alone five." She folded her arms beneath her breasts and stared at them.

"Ah, I've taken care of that," Clint said. He disengaged himself from Mona, walked to the bed, took Jess by the hand and helped her to her feet.

"Hey, what's going on?" Mona demanded.

"Don't worry," he said. "My friend is very big. You won't be disappointed."

He went past them into the hall with Jess in tow. When he turned to close the door, he saw Bigelow smiling at him, and the big man winked.

Clint pulled the door shut and then locked it with the key from the outside.

"What happens if they want to get out?" Jess asked.

"Knowing my friend Sam, I don't think any of the three of them will be looking to get out before morning."

"And what of us?" she asked.

"Ah," he said, "we have our choice of any available room on this floor."

"And will we be locked in?"

"No. Rest assured if you want to get out, the door will be unlocked."

"If I'm any judge of men," she said, taking his hand, "I don't think either one of us will be wanting to get out before morning."

They found an empty room quite close to the room they had just left.

"Do you want to hear the noise they make?" she asked. "Or do you want them to hear the noise we will be making?"

"I just like to keep an eye — or an ear — on my friends."

As they entered the room Jess turned and began to unbutton her shirt. Clint closed the door, and then gave her his full attention as she undressed.

She removed the shirt and was naked beneath it. Her breasts were large, their firmness just beginning to slacken, but not unattractively. Had they been firm and uplifted, it would have given her too perfect a look. Her nipples were large and an oddly pale color.

Next she unbuttoned her pants and slid her thumbs into the waistband, pushing them down over her hips. There was a wisp of fabric covering her pubic hair, but that she quickly discarded. Her hips were firm, her legs long and lean. She turned for him to show him her butt, which was a bit flat. She could have used a few extra pounds in some key areas, but not her breasts. Given the leanness of the rest of her, her breasts looked even larger than they were. Overall, she was a handsome package, and obviously proud of the way she looked.

Clint liked her because she was old enough to be experienced, and young enough to put the experience to good use.

"Now you," she said. She spread her legs and stood with her hands on her hips. She was sucking in her stomach, although it was not at all necessary.

"All right," he said.

For a moment he thought about Bigelow in the other room. Even though he had locked him in, he could have gotten out through the window. At that moment, however, he heard sounds from the other room which indicated that all three parties were still there—and enjoying themselves.

"It sounds as if they've gotten to it very quickly," Jess said. "I like it slow and easy, myself."

"That doesn't strike me as Sam Bigelow's style."

"It wasn't," she said. "Sam was nice, but he's a little too concerned with his own enjoyment."

"You didn't enjoy yourself?"

"Oh, I always manage to enjoy myself, Clint," she said, "but I have a feeling that tonight is going to be . . . special."

"I think I can guarantee that."

"You're not modest," she said. "That's good."

"And I'm not overly concerned about my own pleasure," he said, unbuttoning his shirt. "Oh, I make sure I always enjoy myself, but I also make sure that my . . . partners enjoy themselves, as well."

"This is starting to sound more and more special," she said.

He removed his shirt, shucked his boots and in quick order removed the remainder of his clothing.

"Yes . . ." she said, her eyes drawn to his erect penis. He could see her nipples tightening, and her breathing quickening.

He moved close to her and put his hands lightly on her hips. Her flesh was very hot, and smooth. She closed her eyes as he touched her and took a deep breath. He moved his hands from her hips around to her buttocks. They may have been a little flat, but they felt wonderful. He closed his hands over them and pulled her close to him, so that his penis was trapped between her thighs.

"Ooh," she said, taking her breath in between her teeth, "it's burning hot."

"So are you."

"I'm raging . . ." she said. She lifted her chin and he bent to kiss her. Her lips seared themselves to his, and her tongue flashed into his mouth.

She put her hands on his chest and slid them down his torso, over his belly, until she found him. She closed her hands over his penis, enjoying the smoothness of it in her palms.

"Mmmm," she moaned into his mouth. He slid his hands up from her buttocks along the line of her back and pressed her to him so that her breasts were flattened against his chest. The kiss went on for a very long time, and when it ended she was breathless.

"Oh my," she said.

"Does your husband know where you are?" he asked.

"My husband works all day, then drinks a bottle of whiskey after dinner and goes to bed." She pressed her lips to his neck and said, "He doesn't care where I am."

He moved his hands over her back, enjoying the smoothness of her skin. She was doing the same with his penis, running her hands over it as it swelled even more.

"The bed," she said, kissing his throat. "Now?"

"Now," he agreed.

They moved to the bed together and lowered themselves onto it gently. It creaked, but held. Clint wondered if it was up to what was going to come next.

Once they became thoroughly involved with one another, though, he doubted if they would notice if and when it collapsed.

THIRTY

Sam Bigelow was puzzled.

What was puzzling him was his own reaction in the cantina, when Clint Adams had been facing certain death—a death which would have freed him from the Gunsmith for good.

Why, then, had he thrown that beer mug, giving Clint Adams the edge he needed to survive?

Mona was lying on his right, with one leg tossed over him, and Rosa was on his left, one arm thrown across his chest. Her hand was resting on Mona's right breast, and had been placed there deliberately just before she drifted off to sleep. He'd watched in fascination for a while as the Mexican girl's hand had unconsciously stroked the soft flesh of the breast, while the American girl moaned in her sleep.

These girls were even closer than close friends.

Bigelow guessed that he had helped Clint Adams for the simple reason that he had come to like the man, even though the man held his life in his hands.

That was going to be a problem later, given the fact that he knew he was going to have to kill Clint himself, eventually.

He looked at both girls, wondering which one he should

wake up first—or maybe he should just wake them both and watch for a while.

"I do this a lot," Jess said.
Clint didn't reply.
"I hope you don't mind."
"Why should I mind?" he said.
"Oh, I don't know."
"Your husband doesn't mind, right?"
"He doesn't know."
"He thinks you're beside him in bed all night?"
"If we slept in the same bed he might think that," she said. "But we don't sleep in the same bed."
"You don't?"
"We don't even sleep in the same room," she said.
"Why did you marry him?"
"Because he's safe."
"Safe?"
She nodded.
"He has money, and he makes no demands on me."
"Sexual demands?"
"That's right. All he wants me to do is work in his restaurant waiting tables. At night he drinks himself to sleep, and he doesn't care what I do."
"Doesn't sound like a perfect marriage."
"It's not, but it's probably the closest I'll ever come."
"Why don't you try another town?" he asked. "Another man?"
"Is this a proposal?"
"No."
She laughed.
"I've tried other towns, and other men. Now when I try another man, it's only for one night."
"I see."

"This is only for one night, isn't it?" she asked.

"Oh, yes."

"I mean, you are leaving tomorrow, aren't you?"

"Yes, I am."

"Because I have to tell you," she said, her hand moving down over his belly to grasp his penis, "if you were staying, there is danger that you could become habit-forming."

He cupped one of her breasts and said, "Let's just make sure our one night is a memorable one."

"It has been already," she breathed, "but there's no harm in making sure . . ."

Sam Bigelow watched Mona and Rosa for a while, and they really seemed to enjoy each other. Rosa especially liked it when Mona got down between her legs and licked her like a cat. She was doing that now, and Sam decided that he was a doer, not a watcher.

He got onto the bed with them, positioning himself behind Mona. While she was running her tongue all around Rosa, her ass was hiked up into the air, and she had an exceptionally fine ass. He spread her thighs slightly and slid into her vagina.

She moaned into Rosa's muff, and Rosa suddenly cried out and clutched at Mona's head. Bigelow, excited by the sound of Rosa's completion, rammed into Mona mercilessly until he exploded. He felt her shudder and come and he kept spurting into her, feeling as if he'd never stop . . .

"Why are you leaving?" Clint asked.

Dressing, Jess looked at him and said, "If I don't leave now, you'll have a clinging female on your hands come morning. You don't want that."

He had to agree.

She came to him, dressed now, bent, and kissed him tenderly.

"You spoil a woman, Clint Adams," she said, against his mouth. "You care more for a woman's pleasure than for your own. You're a rare man. Maybe I'll try staying faithful to my husband for a while . . . or at least, until you come back this way."

She hurried to the door and out, and he thought about what she had said about staying faithful.

As much as she obviously exjoyed sex, he was sure that that resolve would last until the next set of broad shoulders came along.

Clint got up and dressed and moved into the hallway. He stopped at the door to Bigelow's room and listened. He heard three distinct voices raised in different tones, all obviously in the throes of pleasure, or pain . . . or both.

It was fairly obvious that the three occupants of the room would be there for some time to come. Clint went back to the room he'd shared with Jess Bates and lay down on the bed fully dressed. Jess's scent filled his nostrils, and he doubted he'd be able to fall asleep . . . right up until the moment that he did.

In the other room Bigelow and the two cantina girls were still going at it.

Mona and Rosa had Bigelow's penis standing stiffer than ever and were both working it with their mouths. They had it wet with their saliva, licking up and down, and when they got to that big, bulging head, their tongues would fence with one another. One time they reached the top together and fell into a real deep, wet kiss, with his spongy head right there between them. It was really something watching two lovely women kiss each other with your penis half in one mouth and half in the other.

When they had worked his penis to the point where it was straining to explode, one girl sat on it, taking it deep inside of her, while the other girl moved up and sat on his face so that he could plunge his tongue deep into her, fucking her that way.

At that point Bigelow didn't know which girl was where, and he didn't rightly care.

It was also at that point in time that he suddenly remembered that underneath that very bed was better than eleven thousand dollars.

THIRTY-ONE

Clint woke with a start. He sat up quickly in bed and took his gunbelt off the bedpost. Standing, he strapped it on. He'd fallen asleep fully dressed, boots and all, so he just walked out into the hallway, used his key to unlock the door of the other room and opened the door. He expected to see Bigelow in bed with both women, but what he saw surprised him.

Sam Bigelow was lying on the bed, buck naked. He was lying on his back and Clint could see that, even flaccid, Bigelow had a cock like a tree, as befitted his size.

That wasn't the surprising part, though.

The surprising part was that he was alone.

"Sam!" Clint said.

Bigleow awoke immediately. Aware of his nakedness, he made no effort to hide it. He turned his head and looked at Clint.

"And how was your night?" he asked.

"Fine," Clint said. "How about yours? I see the ladies decided to leave early."

Bigelow yawned so long and wide that Clint could have sworn he heard the man's jaw crack.

"They wanted to leave early, said something about getting their beauty sleep."

"How'd they get out?"

"I let them out," Bigelow said. He reached for his pants, dug into the pocket and came out with a key.

"You didn't think I'd really let you lock me in here, did you?"

"Why didn't you leave, then?" Clint asked. "The money was under the bed the whole time."

"You know something?" Bigelow said. "Those two gals had me going so much I plumb forgot about the money."

Clint frowned, studying the man. There was a reason Bigelow—and the money—were still around, but he couldn't figure it.

In point of fact, he himself had forgotten that he'd left the money under the bed. That was why he'd woken up with such a start. In a dream, he remembered that the money was under the bed in the room with Bigelow.

"You ready for some breakfast?" Clint asked.

"Ready as I'll ever be, I guess," Bigelow said, scratching his balls and yawning again. "Just let me get dressed."

"I'll wait downstairs."

"I'll be right there," Bigelow said. "Here." He tossed the extra key to Clint. "Give that back to the clerk, will ya?"

Clint looked at the key lying in his palm and shook his head. All along he'd thought that Sam Bigelow was his prisoner.

Maybe that wasn't the way of it at all.

"Maybe we can make this easier on both of us," Clint said to Sam Bigelow.

"How's that?"

They were a half a day out of Bonita, riding south, and had stopped and made camp for some lunch. They were now sitting across the fire from each other, both holding cups of hot coffee.

It had occured to both men that the cup of coffee Bigelow was holding could easily end up in Clint's face, but somehow that never happened.

"You can tell me where the Lanahans are holed up."

"And then what? You'd let me go?"

"I'd consider it."

"Why?"

"That's a good question, Sam," Clint said. "Sort of like why you helped me in the cantina back in town."

"Yep, that's another good question, all right."

"You got an answer for it?"

"No more than you do for yours."

"Right then," Clint said. "What do you say?"

"You're asking me to give up my friends to save myself, Clint," Bigelow said. "Do I strike you as that kind of a man?"

"To tell you the truth, no, you don't, but then maybe I was hoping the Lanahan boys weren't really your friends."

"They ain't," Bigelow said. "Leastways, Kyle and Will ain't."

"Then it's Len Lanahan you rode with?"

"We've ridden together on and off for nigh onto ten years, Clint. He's saved my life more'n I can count, and I've saved his nearly as many. You don't give up a man you been through that with, not that easy, anyway."

"Meaning what?" Clint asked. "If I throw the money in you'll do it?"

Bigelow made a face, the kind of face you make when you're faced with a quandary.

"Ah, I don't think I'd do it even then, Clint," the big man said, "but that don't mean you couldn't try me out on it."

"I don't think I will, Sam."

"Why not?"

"I wouldn't want that on my conscience." Clint tossed the remains of his coffee into the fire and stood up.

"Let's get a move on."

Bigelow paused, then tossed his coffee into the fire, as well.

"You gonna tie my hands?" he asked, standing.

"I don't think so."

"You're getting pretty trustworthy in your old age. Why is that?"

"A man who saves a life doesn't turn around and take it that easily."

"He does if it means saving his own."

"You could have accomplished that back there by minding your own business," Clint said, reminding him. "That is, unless you've got something else in mind."

"Right now I've got it in mind to put out this fire," Bigelow said, kicking dirt onto the flame. Clint joined him and in seconds they had the fire doused and the ashes spread out.

As they started off both men were silent, alone with their own thoughts.

Clint was wondering if he could take this man he had somehow come to like and respect back to Texas and turn him in, knowing he'd most likely hang for what he did.

Bigelow was wondering if, when the time came, he'd be able to do what Clint had said, take a life he had once saved.

Both men were a lot more confused than they had been in recent memory.

THIRTY-TWO

Lola McKay opened her gun shop that morning, thinking about the Lanahan brothers.

She had met them when they first came to town because one of them—Will—had needed his gun repaired. When the three of them walked in she knew they were on the run, but that didn't bother her. Hell, what no one in the town of Angelina knew was that when she first came here five years ago *she* had been on the run herself. In Texas she'd killed her husband when she found him in bed with another woman—in *their* bed, in *their* ranch house. They'd acquitted her for that one, but right after the trial she'd gone and found the bitch he'd been sleeping with and killed *her*. She'd have never got off for that one, so she took her gun and horse and headed for Mexico.

She'd drifted for a while, and then settled in Angelina. She hadn't told Len Lanahan that, yet.

Len was the one she liked, but she'd taken to having sex with all of them. Will was clumsy, but he thought he was really something in bed.

Kyle was sweet, and inexperienced. With some practice he'd become a very good lover.

Maybe as good as Len was.

Lola had had a lot of men since she'd shot her husband.

Back then she swore that a man would never be more to her than a handy penis to slip up between her legs to douse the fire.

She didn't see anything about the Lanahan brothers to change her mind, but she did get a kick out of sleeping with all three of them.

Len knew she was sleeping with both Will and Kyle as well, but both Will and Kyle thought that they were the one she'd picked.

She wondered how they'd react if they found out she was sleeping with all three of them.

It was a dangerous game to play, but somebody had to do it.

Len Lanahan sat in the cantina with a beer in front of him. Doing that comprised half of his days in Angelina, and he didn't mind that. When he wasn't sitting in the cantina—drinking, eating, playing poker with his brothers—he was either sleeping alone in his room, or sleeping with Lola in her room.

Oddly enough, for a man who had seen as much action as he had over the past twenty years, he was content.

His brothers, though; they were a different story.

He knew that both Will and Kyle were bedding Lola, and he marveled at the woman's ability to juggle the three of them. He didn't mind, but he knew that Will and Kyle would go crazy if they found out. They each thought the woman was in love with them, the poor fools!

Aside from Lola, though, there was nothing they liked about the town. He knew they wanted to leave, and he knew that they would all leave sooner or later. The thing he worried about was what would happen when they asked Lola to go with them?

Maybe Will and Kyle would kill each other over her,

and then Len Lanahan would no longer be a prisoner to a promise made to a withering old woman on her deathbed.

"And Kyle is so young."

"I know, Ma."

"They'd die without you."

"I know, Ma."

She'd reached out to him then and he'd taken her bony, almost lifeless hand in his.

"I trust you, Lenny."

"I know, Ma."

"Take care of them for me."

"I will, Ma . . ."

I will Ma, I will Ma, I will Ma . . .

With those three words he had tied himself to these two morons for the rest of his life.

Or the rest of theirs.

THIRTY-THREE

Three days later Clint Adams and Sam Bigelow came to a sign in the road that said: ANGELINA.

"Ever heard of it?" Clint asked Bigelow.

"No."

"Not another rogue town?"

"If it is, I don't know about it."

Clint started Duke forward until Bigelow said, "Hey?"

"What?"

"What do you intend to do, just continue to ride around Mexico until you run into them?"

"What else can I do?" Clint asked. "You won't tell me where they are." There was a pause and then Clint said, "Will you?"

"I can't, Clint," Bigelow said. "I don't know where they are."

"Then we ride."

"You know, they won't be like those four back in Bonita," Bigelow said. "Lenny Lanahan's a good hand with a gun, and he's taught his brothers as much as he can."

"And then there's you, isn't there, Sam?"

"And then there's me."

"But your gun is empty, isn't it?"

Bigelow smiled and said, "Is it?"

Bigelow took his gun out, pointed it into the sky, and fired. A live rounder went rocketing skyward.

Bigelow handed Clint his gun, and Clint emptied it onto the ground and handed it back.

"I'm just showing off," Bigelow said, holstering the gun.

"And very well, too."

"You're not surprised."

"Nothing about you surprises me, Sam. You impress me."

"Ha!" Bigelow said with a smile. "Coming from you that's a great compliment."

"That just means when the time comes, I won't hesitate to kill you," Clint said. "I respect you too much to take chances."

"I see."

"Shall we go now?"

"To Angelina?"

"Unless there is some reason you know of for us not to go there."

Bigelow shrugged and said, "I don't know anything about the place."

"Then let's go."

"After you."

Clint smiled, and urged Duke forward again.

As they rode into Angelina, Lola was looking out her front door. New men in town were an event for her. There hadn't been any since the Lanahans, weeks before.

These two looked interesting, to say the least. One man was tall and slender, riding a magnificent black horse, probably a gelding. The other man was huge, riding a rather ordinary brown horse.

She watched as they rode by, and felt sure that they had both seen her. She *knew* that to men she was interesting-looking, and so assumed that she would be seeing them again—soon.

"Did you see the woman?" Bigelow asked.
"In the doorway of the gunsmith shop?" Clint asked. "Tall, dark-haired, American woman?"
"Yeah."
"I didn't see her."

Angelina was typical of Mexican towns that were too deep in Mexico to command much *gringo* traffic. The arrival of *gringos* was an event—but Mexicans reacted to events the same way they reacted to most afternoons.
Sleepily.
And besides, there were already three *gringos* in town.
Suddenly, it was getting to be old news.
But even old news traveled fast.

"Lenny!"
Kyle came into the cantina quickly.
"Why does he always act like you're the only one who's here?" Will Lanahan asked, annoyed.
"Keep quiet, Will." Len looked at Kyle. "What are you all het up about?"
"The word is two men rode into town today," Kyle said. "*Gringos,* Lenny. Think they're looking for us?"
"No, I don't," Len said. "Every *gringo* who rides into town isn't going to be part of a posse, Kyle."
Kyle frowned.
"Ain't been but these two, Len."

"What are their descriptions?"

"Uh, one tall and thin, but a real big man. The Mexicans are real impressed with him. Huge shoulders, they say, and legs like tree trunks."

"Kyle, who does that sound like to you?"

Kyle stared at his brother and shrugged.

"Will?"

Will grinned and said, "Sounds like Sam, Lenny."

"Yeah," Len Lanahan, frowning, "it sure does sound like Sam . . . but who's he got with him?"

THIRTY-FOUR

"This is hopeless," Sam Bigelow said.

They were in a room at the hotel, having just checked in.

"What is?"

"Gallavanting around Mexico hoping to run into three Americans who will probably kill you the moment you find them."

"And would that upset you?"

"Damn right it would."

"Why?"

Bigelow leaned forward and said, "I'm gonna let you in on a little secret."

"What's that?"

"In my whole life I've only killed one man—no, two men."

"Right," Clint said, "a sheriff and a deputy back in Labyrinth, Texas."

"Hell, no!" Bigelow said. "I never fired a shot that day."

"You didn't?"

"And I didn't ride your friend down, either," Bigelow said. "I wouldn't do that to a defenseless man."

"But Len Lanahan would?"

"Any of the Lanahans would," Bigelow said. "They

don't have my regard for human life."

"Tell me about the two men you *have* killed."

"Oh, them," Bigelow said. "My uncle and my cousin."

"Your *uncle* and your *cousin*?"

Bigelow nodded.

"Why?"

"They were raping my mother," Bigelow said.

"And your father?"

"He was already dead for years. I was eight when he died, and my uncle—my father's brother—took us to live with him. My aunt was alive then, but she died when I was twelve. My cousin was six years older than I was. When I was fourteen I found out that they had been . . . having their way with my mother, as payment to keep us living with them. One night when she was screaming, and they were having at her, I got a gun and killed them both."

There was a moment of silence between them and then Clint said, "I'd say they got what they deserved."

"They got better than they deserved," Bigelow said. "They died quick."

"*If* the story is true."

Bigelow's head jerked up and he glared at Clint.

"I wouldn't lie about a thing like that."

"If you're telling the truth, Sam—about Labyrinth, I mean—in the eyes of the law you're still as guilty as the Lanahans."

"And in your eyes?"

"I want the men who actually shot and rode down my friend," Clint said. "The men who killed the sheriff and the deputy. If you help me get them, then you can go free."

Bigelow didn't reply.

"Are you and Len Lanahan such good friends—"

"I never said we was good friends," Bigelow said. "I said we rode together a long time, and worked together a long time. That doesn't mean that we're friends."

"Then you'll help me find them.?"

"I'll help you find them," Sam Bigelow said, "but I won't help you kill them."

"I want to take them back with me."

"You'll have to kill them, Clint," Bigelow said. "They won't go back with you."

"We'll see," Clint said. "For now let's see if we can't get something to eat."

"Uh, I wouldn't just go walking out on the street if I was you."

"Why not?"

"Because they're here."

Clint stared at Bigelow.

"The Lanahans?"

Bigelow nodded.

"Are here?"

He nodded again.

"And you knew they were here?"

"No," Bigelow said. "I saw their horses in the livery stable. That means their horses are here, which means they were here and possibly still are here. *Probably* still are here."

"Well, even if they are they don't know me," Clint said.

"They do know me," Bigelow said. "By now they know I'm here, and they know that you're with me."

"So?"

"So we'll have to stick together," Bigelow said. "They'll want to know who you are."

"And what will we tell them?"

"Damned if I know," Bigelow said, "but we'll have to figure out something."

"Well, let's figure it out over lunch, huh?"

"Sure."

Clint started for the door and Bigelow said, "Oh, one more thing."

"What?"

"I'll need some bullets for my gun."

Clint stared at Bigelow, who waited expectantly.

"You gotta trust somebody, Clint."

"All right," Clint said, finally. "We'll go to the gunsmith's and get some."

"Before lunch?"

Clint nodded and said, "Before lunch."

When they walked into the gun shop, Lola McKay was standing behind the counter. She studied both of them boldly as they approached. They also studied her.

She saw two attractive men in their early forties, each in his own way in excellent physical condition.

They saw a dark-haired beauty of a woman in her early thirties, very tall, with broad shoulders and hips and full breasts.

"We need some bullets," Bigelow said.

"What caliber?"

Clint remained silent while Bigelow told her what kind of bullets they needed. When the time came to pay, Clint took out the money and handed it to her.

"Thank you," she said. Her fingers brushed his hand before she took the money from him.

Bigelow loaded his gun before they left the shop.

"You boys just passing through?" she asked.

"That's right," Clint said.

"You'll be staying overnight, though."

"Yes," Clint said, matching the boldness of her gaze, "at least overnight."

"Well . . ." she said, "good . . . if I can help you with . . . anything else, please let me know."

"You could tell us a good place to eat," Bigelow said.

Since she was apparently more interested in Clint, Bigelow was more interested in food.

"There is a small cafe just down the block," she said. "They make excellent Mexican food, and could probably make a decent steak, if you prefer."

"That sounds good to me," Bigelow said, holstering his newly loaded gun. "Shall we go—" Bigelow said to Clint, and stopped just short of calling him by name. "Shall we go?"

"Yes," Clint said. "Thank you for your help, Miss—"

"McKay, Lola McKay," she said. "You can call me Lola."

"Lola," he said, nodding.

"And you . . ."

"His name is Sam," Clint said, "and my name is . . . Adam."

"Pleased to meet both of you," she said. "Enjoy Angelina," she said. "It's small and sleepy, but it does have some . . . attractions."

"So I've noticed," Clint said.

"Adam?" Bigelow said. "Can we get going? I'm kind of hungry."

"Yes," Clint said, staring at Lola's big brown eyes, "so am I . . ."

Bigelow took hold of Clint's arm and led him from the gunsmith shop.

"After this is over we go our separate ways," Bigelow said over lunch. He was having a steak, claiming that the one thing he missed the most about being away from the U.S. was American food.

Clint was eating Mexican food.

"Why do you say that?" he asked.

"Too many women find you . . . interesting."

"It's my charm," Clint said. "It's why I don't pay for my pleasure."

"It's that look you carry."

"What look?"

"The look of a man who is going to die a violent death," Bigelow said. "It attracts them like flies."

"Is that a fact?" Clint said. "And I have that look, do I?"

"I have it, you have it, Lenny Lanahan has it. You've lived a violent life, Clint, as have I," Bigelow said. "Your reputation is proof of that. Men who live a violent life should expect to die a violent death. I know I do."

Clint thought for a moment of Bill Hickok, killed by an assassin's bullet fired from behind.

"Yes," he said, "I do, too, someday—but not someday soon."

"None of us intend it to be someday soon," Bigelow said. "Unfortunately, we don't have any control over that, do we?"

"No," Clint agreed, "we sure don't."

THIRTY-FIVE

"If it is Sam, what's he doing here?" Will Lanahan asked. "And who's the fella with him?"

"We'll have to ask him that, won't we?" Len Lanahan said to his brother.

"Let's go, Lenny," Will said, standing up. "Let's go and ask him."

"You do that, Will," Len said. "You go and find him and ask him."

"Me?" Will said. Rubbing his palms on his shirt he asked, "Why me?"

"Because I'm telling you to."

"Aw, Len, you know Sam don't like me," Will Lanahan said, wetting his lips. "He'd as soon kill me as look at me. You know that. Why don't you send Kyle."

"I'll go," Kyle said, a sneer in his voice which was meant for Will. "I ain't afraid of Sam."

"Then you're stupid," Len said. "You *should* be afraid of Sam Bigelow. He could break you in two without breaking a sweat."

"Len—"

"You go, Will," Lanahan said. "You're less likely to say something to piss Sam off."

"Len—"

"Go ahead!"

Reluctantly, Will Lanahan left the cantina and went to find Sam Bigelow and the man he had ridden in with.

"Why didn't you let me go—" Kyle started to complain.

"Shut up, Kyle!" Len snapped. "Go to the door and keep an eye out."

"For what?"

"For anything."

Kyle went over to the door and looked out at the street, sulking.

Len Lanahan couldn't figure out what would bring Sam Bigelow to Angelina. When they'd parted company, Sam was on his way back to Texas. Now he was here with another man, and Len didn't think Sam was back because he missed the Lanahans.

Something was up, and he meant to find out what.

Nervously, Will Lanahan went to the hotel to see if Sam Bigelow was there. The Lanahans had left the hotel and were staying in rooms above the cantina.

Will saw that Bigelow had signed in the register book, but that the man with him had not.

"Do you know where they went?" he asked the clerk.

"I heard them say they had to buy bullets, *señor*," the clerk said.

"Thanks, Pepe."

Will didn't like the idea of looking for Bigelow, but at least he'd get to see Lola.

"Yeah, they were here," Lola said.

"Do you know where they were going from here, Lola?" Will asked.

RIDE FOR VENGEANCE 159

"Sure, down the street to get something to eat. What's going on, Will? Are these men friends of yours and your brothers'?"

"Yeah, honey," Will said, patting her hand. "They're friends of ours. Thanks."

As Will left, Lola wondered what was going on. She'd never seen him so nervous—or scared!

Will Lanahan paused outside the cafe to dry his sweaty palms on his shirt.

He had always hated Sam Bigelow because he feared the big man. He also hated him becuase Will knew that his brother Lenny would rather have ridden with Bigelow than with him, and it was only because of his promise to their mother that Lenny kept him and Kyle with him.

Will wished he had the nerve to kill Sam Bigelow, and prove to his brother that he was as good as—or better than—Bigelow was.

He took a deep breath and entered the cafe.

THIRTY-SIX

"Get ready," was all Sam Bigelow had time to say to Clint Adams when Will Lanahan entered the cafe.

Bigelow and Clint watched Lanahan approach the table with small steps, as if he could think of a million other things he'd rather do.

"Hello, Sam," he finally said.

"Will."

"I—uh, we didn't expect to see you here," Will said. "Last we knew you were headed for Texas."

"I didn't expect to see you here either, Will," Bigelow said. "I didn't know you and your brothers were in Angelina. Your brothers are with you, aren't they?"

"Oh, sure," Will said, "Kyle and Lenny, they're here."

"Where?" Bigelow asked.

"What?"

Bigelow closed his eyes and then opened them. Clint thought the man was having a hard time being patient with Will Lanahan.

"Where are they?"

"Oh, they're over at the cantina. We got some rooms right upstairs from it."

"I see," Bigelow said. "Lenny send you over here to talk to me?"

"Uh, sure, yeah, he did."

"Why didn't he come himself?"

Will shrugged.

"I don't know," Will said. "I guess he was busy."

"Did he look busy the last time you saw him, Will?" Bigelow asked.

"Uh, no, he was just sitting—well, yeah, he was kind of busy . . . I guess . . ."

"Will, you tell Lenny I'll be over to talk to him in a little while."

"Yeah, well, see, he sent me over to find out, uh, why you're—"

"You go and tell him what I said."

Will hesitated, because he obviously was not getting done what his brother had told him to get done.

He decided to give it one more try.

"Uh, who's this feller, Sam?"

"Will."

"Yeah, Sam?"

"Get out of here and let me finish my lunch in peace."

"Aw, Sam, you hadn't ought to talk to me—"

Bigelow made a move as if to rise and suddenly Will Lanahan was backing toward the door. When he backed into the wall near the door he rolled off it and ran out the door.

"He's about as afraid of you as one man can be of another," Clint observed.

"He's an idiot," Bigelow said. "Of the three he's the one I have the least use for."

"And the younger one? Kyle?"

"He's still got time to turn out right, if Lenny can teach him. Lord knows, Lenny could never teach Will anything. I don't know how much luck he'll have with Kyle."

"Not much," Clint said, "if I take them back to Texas with me."

"There's that, yeah," Bigelow said. "You know, I can't swear to it, Clint, but I'm pretty sure it was Will who shot your friend and rode him down."

"But you can't swear to it."

"No," Bigelow said, "no, I can't . . . but I'm pretty sure."

"Maybe we'll be able to find out for sure."

"Maybe," Bigelow said, "but don't expect Len Lanahan to give up one of his brothers so easily."

"I don't expect any man to give up his brother easily, Sam," Clint said, and then added, "or his friend."

"Let's finish our lunch," Sam Bigelow said, "and then I'll take you over to see Lenny."

Clint Adams wondered how much of a mistake he was making, trusting Sam Bigelow to even the smallest extent. He had run into likable rogues before—and likable killers, as well. There was no denying that Sam Bigelow was a likable man, and that the man had saved his life, but when it came down to Clint or the Lanahans—specifically Len Lanahan—Clint just couldn't predict which way the big man would go.

As much as Bigelow claimed that he and Len Lanahan were partners, but not necessarily friends, there was a bond that formed between men who rode together for a length of time.

How strong that bond was between Bigelow and Len Lanahan was something Clint Adams was going to find out for himself, very soon.

THIRTY-SEVEN

"You're an idiot, Will."

"You shouldn't say things like that to me, Len," Will Lanahan said, sitting down opposite his older brother. "What would Maw say?"

"Ma's the one who told me you were an idiot," Len said to Will.

Will gaped as Kyle started to laugh.

"What the hell are you laughing at?" Len said.

"Uh, I don't—uh, Len—" Kyle stammered.

"You're at least as much of an idiot as he is," Len went on. "Do you know the only difference between you and him?"

"Uh, no—"

"You're younger, and you have time to try and overcome your handicap—"

"Aw, Len—"

"When Sam and his new friend come in here, I don't want to hear a word out of either one of you. Have you got that?"

Neither Will nor Kyle answered.

"I said, have you got that!"

"Yes," Kyle said.

"Not a word," Will said. "We'll do just like you say, Len."

"If you do, it'll be a goddamned first!"

Len Lanahan was puzzled, and he was taking it out on his brothers. Actually, shouting at them that way—the way he'd wanted to for a long time—made him feel a little better.

He'd feel a lot better when he found out why Sam Bigelow was in Angelina, and who the man with him was.

"All right," he said to his chastised brothers, "make damn sure nobody else comes in here until Sam gets here."

Both Will and Kyle got up and moved to the door.

As Clint and Bigelow approached the cantina Sam Bigelow asked, "Who's going to do the talking?"

"You introduce me," Clint said, "and then I'll do the talking."

"Introduce you as who?"

"As who I am," Clint said. "I'm not going to keep any secrets from the Lanahan boys."

"Do you think that's wise?"

"Do you think I could trick them back to Texas?"

"No."

"Then we'll try the truth."

"It's your neck . . ."

"Here they come, Len," Will said.

"Go sit in a corner," Len Lanahan said.

"Len—" Kyle started.

"Both of you!"

Both brothers went to separate corners and sat at a table.

The batwing doors of the cantina opened, and Sam Bigelow entered, with another man who Len Lanahan did not know.

Yet.

RIDE FOR VENGEANCE 167

• • •

"Hello, Len."

"Hello, Sam."

It was very quiet in the cantina.

"Who's your friend, Sam?" Len Lanahan asked.

"He's not my friend, Len."

"Then what?"

"A man who had an interest in finding you."

"What interest?"

"I'll let him tell it."

"What's his name, this man who had an interest?"

"Clint Adams," Sam Bigelow said, and fell silent.

The rest was up to the Gunsmith.

Clint Adams stepped forward.

"I know who you are, Adams," Len Lanahan said. "What interest do you have in me?"

"I've come to take you and your brothers back to Texas, Lanahan."

"For what?"

"To stand trial for what you did in Labyrinth."

Len Lanahan frowned, as if trying to think, to remember.

"Labyrinth?" he said. "What did I do in Labyrinth?"

"You—and your brothers—are wanted for bank robbery and murder. More important to me, however, is the fact that you shot a friend of mine, and then rode over him."

"Is he dead, this friend of yours?"

"No," Clint said, "not the last I heard."

"Then he can identify the man who shot him and rode him down."

"Yes."

"And you intend to take us back and give him a good look at us, eh?"

"Him, and the people from the bank."

"All by yourself?"

Clint looked at Sam Bigelow, and the big man looked away.

"If I have to."

"Against the four of us?" Len Lanahan asked. He looked at Sam Bigelow, and the big man looked away. "Against the three of us?"

"If that's the way it must be."

Len Lanahan studied the man standing before him, the man claiming to be Clint Adams, the Gunsmith.

"Have you any legal standing?" he asked. "Are you . . . a lawman?"

"No," Clint said, "and even if I was, I wouldn't have any legal standing here in Mexico."

"Then how do you hope to take us back?"

"Maybe I'll be able to persuade you to return with me."

Len Lanahan laughed.

"To a hangman's rope?"

"To a fair trial."

Len Lanahan looked at each of his brothers in turn.

"What say you boys to a fair trial?"

It took them a moment each to realize that he wanted an answer.

"Uh, no, Len," Will said.

"No, Lenny," Kyle said.

"My brothers have spoken, Adams," Len Lanahan said. "And what about you, Sam? You stand to have your neck stretched, as well."

"I didn't kill anyone," the big man said.

"Ha!" Len Lanahan laughed. He looked at Clint and said, "Is that what he told you?"

Clint didn't answer.

"I don't know what he's told you, but he's killed more men than the three of us put together," Lanahan said, waving his arms to encompass his brothers and himself.

"Not in Labyrinth," Sam Bigelow said.

That answer did not sit well with Clint. It was contrary to what Bigelow had told him.

"Come back with me," Clint Adams said.

"You'll have to take us back, Adams," Len Lanahan said, "because we won't go with you willingly."

"Tomorrow, then," Clint said. "Be ready to leave tomorrow."

"But we can kill him now, Len," Will Lanahan said aloud.

"Tomorrow will be soon enough, Will," Len said.

"But Len—" Kyle said.

"Be quiet," Len said softly. He turned his attention to Clint and said, "We'll see you tomorrow, Adams."

Clint nodded and backed toward the door, unsure as to whether or not Sam Bigelow would follow.

"Stay for a drink, Sam," Len Lanahan said. "A drink with an old friend."

Sam Bigelow looked at Clint Adams for a moment, then back to Len Lanahan.

"Sure, Lenny," the big man said.

"Unless you are joined with Adams."

Bigelow hesitated and then said, "I'll have a beer."

Clint left the cantina, leaving the two old colleagues to talk.

THIRTY-EIGHT

"Saving yourself, Sam?"

Sam Bigelow took a swallow of his beer and stared across the table at Len Lanahan.

"It didn't start out that way," Bigelow said, "but he's got my money, and Yates'."

"And Yates?"

"He's dead."

"And he took your money?"

"Yes."

"And why aren't you dead, Sam?"

"You of all people should know I'm not that easy to kill, Len."

"Did you offer him us for your freedom?"

"I wasn't in any position to make any offer," Bigelow said.

"Is he really Clint Adams?" Lanahan asked. "Is he really the Gunsmith?"

"He is."

"Did you see him in action?"

"I did."

"Against how many?"

Bigelow hesitated just a beat and then said, "Four."

"And he beat them?"

"They're all dead," Bigelow said.

Lanahan rubbed his jaw.

"This could be interesting."

"Len—" Will said.

"Lenny—" Kyle said.

"Quiet!"

Len Lanahan leaned across the table and stared at Sam Bigelow.

"Where will you stand tomorrow, Sam?" he asked. "With us, or with him?"

Bigelow finished his beer and set the empty mug down. He pushed back his chair and stood up.

"I'll see you tomorrow, Len," he said. He gave both Will and Kyle a glance that turned their blood cold, and then left the cantina.

"Lenny?" Will siad.

"It'll be the three of us against the Gunsmith," Len Lanahan said.

"Can we . . . beat him?"

"Of course we can," Lanahan said.

Or rather, he thought, I can. And when it's over, maybe I'll be rid of an old promise made to an old woman.

"Will," he called, "get me another beer."

"Yes, Len," Will said, rising from his corner.

"We'll join you," Kyle said, rising from his corner.

"No," Len said, "you and your brother get some rest, Kyle. No beer, no whiskey . . . and no Lola. I want you both fresh!"

Fresh to die, Len Lanahan thought, so that I can finally live.

THIRTY-NINE

Lola left her rooms above her shop that night and went to the hotel. Therefore, she was not in her rooms when Len Lanahan showed up there. He used his key to enter to wait for her, and fell asleep in her empty bed.

Clint lay in his bed in the hotel, wondering what tomorrow would bring. He hadn't spoken to Sam Bigelow since he'd left the big man in the cantina with the Lanahan brothers. When tomorrow came would he once again be a colleague of theirs? Or would he stand with Clint Adams?

Or would he stand alone?

There was a knock on his door then, too timid to be Sam Bigelow's.

He stood up, clad only in his britches. No shirt, no boots. His gun was hanging on the bedpost, but he left it there as he went to answer the door.

When he opened it, he saw Lola McKay standing in the hall.

"I heard that there will be some trouble tomorrow," she said.

"Is that the word?"

She nodded.

"Then I guess it's true."

She smiled and asked, "Could you use some . . . distraction tonight?"

"What about the Lanahan brothers?"

She entered the room and put her hand on his bare chest. Her fingertips made circles there and she said, "Let them find their own distractions."

He put his hand on her slim waist and said, "Yes . . ."

He was standing at the window looking out when she woke up. He was naked, and she came up behind him, as naked as he was.

"What are you thinking about?" she asked, pressing her firm breasts against his back. Her nipples were hard, tickling the skin of his back. Her hands came around him, one from beneath his left arm, one from over his right shoulder, and rubbed his chest.

"Just thinking."

"About tomorrow?" she asked, her lips against his back.

"It's today, now."

First light was about fifteen minutes away.

He'd been standing there thinking about the Lanahans. He knew there was no way to take the three of them back to Texas with him. He knew he was going to have to kill them to keep from being killed.

And he knew that he'd brought himself to this point.

"You could leave, you know," she said. "Just get on your horse and ride out."

"I could," he said, "but I can't. I've come this far, I've got to take it to its logical conclusion."

"Come back to bed," she said. "There's time . . ."

"Time for what?" he asked, grinning a little.

She kissed his back, between his shoulder blades, and then continued down, tracing the line of his back with her mouth until she came to his buttocks.

He felt her hot mouth and wet tongue tracing over the contours of his ass, and then she was kissing the backs of his thighs. He braced his hands against the window as her lips brushed over his legs lightly, until she reached the flesh of his inner thigh. Her tongue came out again, licking him, wetting him. She moved around so that she was sitting on the floor between his legs, facing the opposite way. From there she was able to reach his balls, taking them gently into her mouth, and then licking the underside of his shaft as it swelled larger and longer. When she reached the head she took it in her mouth and he backed up a few steps so she could suck him, and ride him up and down with her mouth, and when she had him to the point where he was near exploding she whispered against him, "Come back to bed . . . there's time . . ."

He didn't ask time for what, this time.

When Len Lanahan woke in Lola's bed he sat up and said aloud, "Bitch!"

He knew she wouldn't have gone to Will or Kyle, and he doubted that she would have gone to Sam. That meant she went to Clint Adams.

"Son of a bitch!" he swore, and left to go and wake his brothers.

"Is it time?" Lola asked.

Clint was dressed and wearing his gun.

"It's time," he said, stroking her face.

"Three against one?"

"I guess so."

"What about your big friend?"

"I don't know about him."

"He rode in with you."

"Not by choice."

"Oh," she said. "Is there a chance that he might stand against you?"

"There's a chance," Clint said. "Hell, there's a good chance."

"Look," she said, taking hold of his arm, "I can shoot a rifle."

"No . . ."

"I can stay up here and cover you from the window."

"No!" he said. He pulled his arm free gently and cupped her chin. "Why would you do that? You've known the Lanahans longer than you've known me."

"Maybe longer," she said, "but probably not better. They don't talk to a woman, all they do is grunt and groan over her. Even Len—who's pretty good at the grunting and groaning—he doesn't treat a woman like a woman. No man does . . . except you."

"I'm not the only one."

"You're the only one I ever met," she said. "You don't know this, but I was married once."

"Once? Did he die?"

"He did," she said. "I killed him."

He frowned at her and she told him the story of how she'd killed her husband, and after being acquitted how she'd found the woman he'd been with and killed her. By the time she finished, he was sitting next to her on the bed and she was hugging his arm, pressing her cheek against it.

"Why did you tell me all that?" he asked.

"I don't rightly know," she said. She moved her face away from his arm and left it wet. "I guess I been wanting to tell someone for a long time."

He leaned over and kissed her forehead, then stood up.

"Clint?"

"Yes?"

"I don't know about the Lanahans," she said, "but I'd go back to Texas with you, if you asked me."

"I know you would, honey," he said—and there was no statute of limitations on murder. She'd hang just as sure as the Lanahans would.

If he took her back.

And if he took them back.

FORTY

When Clint left the hotel he saw Sam Bigelow standing across the street. He walked until he was standing in front of the man. Bigelow was standing on the boardwalk and Clint in the street, so the big man towered over him even more than usual.

" 'Morning, Sam."

"Clint."

"Have you decided how you're going to play it?"

Bigelow shrugged.

"Maybe you figure we'll all kill each other and you'll get to walk off with all the money."

"Maybe . . ." Bigelow said. "Have you decided how you're going to play it?"

"Well, something somebody told me a little while ago has just about decided me to give it up and forget about them."

"Really?" Bigelow said, looking genuinely surprised. "I didn't think there was anything anybody could have told you to make you decide that."

"Well, I did decide that . . . but only for a minute."

"What decided you back again?"

"Well, I decided that the two incidents just weren't the same thing. The killing of the two lawmen, that had to be planned, because they had to have known that there'd be law to oppose them."

"And the shooting of your friend?"

"Well, that was just a blatant disregard for human life," Clint said. "Like riding him down afterward. That was just pure mean."

"I guess so."

"So I guess I'll just have to go ahead with it and take them back."

"I guess you will."

"There's only one thing I'm unsure about."

"What's that?"

"You," Clint said. "I'm just not sure which way you're going to go, Sam, so I'll take your gun now."

"What?"

"Your gun," Clint said. "Hand it over."

"You're plannin' on takin' me back, too?"

"I'm planning on removing any temptation from your path," Clint said. "You can have it back after."

"If you're alive after."

"If I'm not," Clint said, "you can take it off my body—and the money's in my hotel room."

The two men exchanged glances for a long moment, and then Bigelow sighed, removed his gun from his holster, and handed it to Clint, butt first. Clint accepted it and tucked it into the front of his belt.

"Thanks, Sam."

"Good luck," Bigelow said. "Watch Len. He's fast."

"I'll remember."

Clint turned and started walking to the cantina.

"You boys understand what I'm telling you?" Len Lanahan asked.

"We understand, Len," Will said, and Kyle nodded.

"One of you on each side of me, and you keep your eyes on me. When I move, you move. Got it?"

"We've got it, Len," Kyle said.

"Take a look outside, Will."

Will went to the window, looked outside, and shouted, "He's comin'!"

"All right," Len said. "Let's go out and meet him."

As Clint was approaching the cantina, the doors opened and the three Lanahan brothers stepped out. As he had figured, Len was in the center.

"You boys ready to ride back to Texas?" Clint asked.

"As a matter of fact, we are," Len Lanahan said, "over your dead body."

Clint was a little surprised that it happened so fast. Len Lanahan reached for his gun, but his hand stopped short of the butt.

Will and Kyle, watching Len for their cue, moved when he did, and they *did* grab their guns.

Clint wondered why the man would set his own brothers up to be killed like that? The only way he could see to keep from killing them was to shoot Len anyway, even though he hadn't grabbed his gun.

Clint drew and fired and Len Lanahan staggered back, a look of shock on his face. Apparently, he'd expected Clint to shoot the two men who *had* actually grabbed their guns.

As for Will and Kyle, when they saw Len go down they forgot all about their guns.

"Lenny!" Will shouted.

He and Kyle both rushed to their brother, who was lying on his back, half in and half out of the cantina.

"All right, boys," Clint said, "toss your guns out here into the street."

Kyle looked at Clint, and then threw his gun into the street.

"Will, come on!" he said to his brother.

Will Lanahan did likewise, tossing his gun into the street.

Clint felt Sam Bigelow come up alongside of him.

"Did you see that?" he asked the big man.

"I did."

"Do you think they know what he did?" Clint said.

"No," Bigelow said, "and they're too dumb to figure it out unless you tell them."

"Why would he want me to kill his brothers?"

"It's a long story," Bigelow said. "Let's just say he got tired of carrying them. Can I have my gun, please?"

Clint looked at Bigelow, then took the man's gun from his belt and handed it over with his left hand. Bigelow took it, and holstered it.

"What do I get to take with me?" Bigelow asked.

"Your horse."

"That's all?"

"It's all I've got to give you, Sam."

Bigelow studied Clint for a moment, then nodded and said, "All right, Clint. I'll take it." He started away, then stopped and asked, "Did you kill him?"

"No," Clint said. "I'll patch him up and take the three of them back to Texas."

"With Len wounded, I don't think you'll have any trouble from the other two."

"I don't anticipate any."

"Clint?"

"Yeah?"

"I hope your friend is still alive when you get there."

Clint looked at Sam Bigelow and then said, "Yeah, so do I," as the big man started walking away.

"And Sam," Clint said.

"Yeah?" Bigelow said, stopping.

Without looking at him Clint said, "If I find out you lied to me about what happened in Labyrinth, I'll be back."

For a moment Clint wondered if the man was still there, he was so quiet, and then Sam Bigelow said, "I know that, Clint."

Clint nodded, said, "Just so you do," and then mounted the boardwalk to round up his prisoners.

Watch For

THE TAKERSVILLE SHOOT

eighty-eighth novel in the exciting
GUNSMITH Series

coming in April!

Lyons Public Library
448 Cedar St.
P.O. Box 100
Lyons, OR 97358

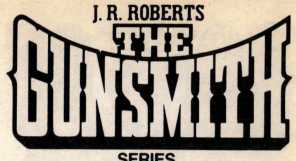

J. R. ROBERTS
THE GUNSMITH
SERIES

☐ 0-441-30932-1	THE GUNSMITH #1:	MACKLIN'S WOMEN	$2.95
☐ 0-441-30930-5	THE GUNSMITH #7:	THE LONGHORN WAR	$2.50
☐ 0-441-30931-3	THE GUNSMITH #11:	ONE-HANDED GUN	$2.50
☐ 0-441-30905-4	THE GUNSMITH #15:	BANDIT GOLD	$2.50
☐ 0-441-30907-0	THE GUNSMITH #17:	SILVER WAR	$2.50
☐ 0-441-30949-6	THE GUNSMITH #45:	NAVAHO DEVIL	$2.50
☐ 0-441-30952-6	THE GUNSMITH #48:	ARCHER'S REVENGE	$2.50
☐ 0-441-30955-0	THE GUNSMITH #51:	DESERT HELL	$2.50
☐ 0-441-30956-9	THE GUNSMITH #52:	THE DIAMOND GUN	$2.50
☐ 0-441-30957-7	THE GUNSMITH #53:	DENVER DUO	$2.50
☐ 0-441-30958-5	THE GUNSMITH #54:	HELL ON WHEELS	$2.50
☐ 0-441-30959-3	THE GUNSMITH #55:	THE LEGEND MAKER	$2.50
☐ 0-441-30964-X	THE GUNSMITH #60:	GERONIMO'S TRAIL	$2.50

Please send the titles I've checked above. Mail orders to:

BERKLEY PUBLISHING GROUP
390 Murray Hill Pkwy., Dept. B
East Rutherford, NJ 07073

NAME _____
ADDRESS _____
CITY _____
STATE _____ ZIP _____

Please allow 6 weeks for delivery.
Prices are subject to change without notice.

POSTAGE & HANDLING:
$1.00 for one book, $.25 for each additional. Do not exceed $3.50

BOOK TOTAL	$_____
SHIPPING & HANDLING	$_____
APPLICABLE SALES TAX (CA, NJ, NY, PA)	$_____
TOTAL AMOUNT DUE PAYABLE IN US FUNDS. (No cash orders accepted.)	$_____

SONS OF TEXAS

Book one in the exciting new saga of America's Lone Star state!

TOM EARLY

Texas, 1816. A golden land of opportunity for anyone who dared to stake a claim in its destiny...and its dangers...

☐ *SONS OF TEXAS*   0-425-11474-0 $3.95

Look for each new book in the series!

B Berkley

Please send the titles I've checked above. Mail orders to:

BERKLEY PUBLISHING GROUP
390 Murray Hill Pkwy., Dept. B
East Rutherford, NJ 07073

NAME _____
ADDRESS _____
CITY _____
STATE _____ ZIP _____

Please allow 6 weeks for delivery.
Prices are subject to change without notice.

POSTAGE & HANDLING:
$1.00 for one book, $.25 for each additional. Do not exceed $3.50.

BOOK TOTAL	$____
SHIPPING & HANDLING	$____
APPLICABLE SALES TAX (CA, NJ, NY, PA)	$____
TOTAL AMOUNT DUE	$____
PAYABLE IN US FUNDS. (No cash orders accepted.)	

185